**It wasn't her thinness that brought
a lump to the therapist's throat.
It was her sadness.**

"I thought being out of the hospital would make a difference," said Kessa.

"You thought you would be cured and happy?"

How did he know that's just what she'd been thinking? Kessa turned down the corners of her mouth and nodded vigorously. "When do I get to feel better?"

Sandy leaned back and waited.

"Why do I hate it when people tell me I look 'so much better'?" She mimicked her mother's voice. "And when will I stop feeling so fat?" She smacked her thighs.

"You are five-foot-four and one hundred and two pounds. There's no room for any part of you to be fat at those proportions. What's really wrong?"

"I don't know how to live." Kessa surprised herself with the blunt honesty of that statement. Tears welled in he_____ Tears she didn't want her therapist to s___

Ple___
for the medical pro_____
enthusiastic response to *Kessa*.

"A great story; a state-of-the-art, exciting presentation of the best treatment of eating disorders ever written for professional and lay audiences. A moving insight into the life of a conflicted young person, all wrapped up into one book. What an exciting feat! What a rich contribution to parents, school people, mental health professionals and physicians who care for our young, fearful-of-adulthood people."

> —Samuel C. Klagsbrun, M.D.
> Medical Director, Four Winds Hospital
> Katonah, New York;
> Associate Clinical Professor in Psychiatry
> Columbia University College of
> Physicians and Surgeons

* * *

"An absorbing book. Steven Levenkron has again demonstrated the sensitivity, patience and insight that have assured his role as a first-class psychotherapist and a leader in the field of eating disorders."

> —John Adams Atchley, M.D.
> Diplomate, American Board of
> Psychiatry and Neurology;
> Assistant Professor of Psychiatry
> Columbia University College of
> Physicians and Surgeons

* * *

"A fascinating story by a man who listens carefully to girls and women."

> —Virginia Pomeranz, M.D.
> Associate Clinical Professor of Pediatrics
> Cornell University Medical College;
> Coauthor of *Mothers' & Fathers'*
> *Medical Encyclopedia*

* * *

"With the sensitivity we have come to expect from Steven Levenkron, he takes further risks in *Kessa*, sharing with us more of what he knows about the treatment process, about eating disorders, and about women. In so doing, he has touched all of us: therapists, patients, families and friends. Thank goodness we are not alone in facing this illness. In troubled times we can return to *Kessa* for solace."

—April Benson, Ph.D.
Director of Training
Center for the Study of Anorexia
Nervosa and Bulimia, N.Y.C.

ABOUT THE AUTHOR

Author of *The Best Little Girl in the World* and *Treating and Overcoming Anorexia Nervosa,* Steven Levenkron is one of the country's foremost experts on anorexia nervosa. In addition to running a full-time private practice in New York City, he is adjunct director of The Eating Disorders Service at Four Winds Hospital in Katonah, New York, and is clinical consultant at the Center for the Study of Anorexia/Bulimia in New York City. He is also a member of the Advisory Board of the National Association of Anorexia Nervosa and Associated Disorders. Steven Levenkron has been treating anorexics since 1970.

Also by
STEVEN LEVENKRON

The Best Little Girl in the World
Treating and Overcoming Anorexia Nervosa

Kessa

Steven Levenkron

POPULAR LIBRARY

An Imprint of Warner Books, Inc.

A Warner Communications Company

Acknowledgments

I would like to thank my agents, George and Olga Wieser, for their professional encouragement and the endurance of the aggravation inherent in being one's agent; I would also like to thank Bernard Shir-Cliff, editor-in-chief of Warner Books, for his faith in the development of this book. Finally, I wish to thank Karen Moline, for her invaluable editorial assistance.

POPULAR LIBRARY EDITION

Popular Library® is a registered trademark of Warner Books, Inc.

Popular Library books are published by
Warner Books, Inc.
666 Fifth Avenue
New York, N.Y. 10103

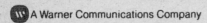 A Warner Communications Company

Printed in the United States of America

First Printing: January, 1986

10 9 8 7 6 5 4 3 2 1

For my wife, Abby
without whose love, support and wisdom
all this would not have been possible.

Chapter
1

The breakfast tray remained untouched. Kessa pushed it away and she moved to the edge of her bed, gazing morosely out the window. She hadn't wanted to come to this crummy hospital anyway, where she knew they'd make her fat. So what was the big deal about going home?

"You sure don't seem happy about getting out of this dump," her roommate, Lila, challenged her. "I can't wait to get home. Means I'm gettin' *better*."

Kessa shrugged, keeping her back to Lila. *Better*, she thought. *Fatter*, you mean. I'm going home to get even more fat than I am now.

"Whatsa matter, cat got your tongue?"

"You're picking on me, as usual. All you ever do is pick on me." Lila always seemed to know what Kessa was thinking.

Lila bit her lower lip. Maybe she did pick on that skinny girl, but she just couldn't stand listening to her say she was fat. When she wasn't.

"Yeah, well maybe I'm picking on you because everything that makes other people happy makes you feel dumb. Eating

1

gives you the creeps. So what if you did gain some weight, girl? You just about died, 'member? And you only gained that weight 'cause they stuck you on that machine with those tubes sticking in you and everything. It's not like you ever ate anything extra your own self. It's—"

"Why don't you just leave me alone, damnit!" Kessa couldn't bear to hear it one more time.

Lila pouted. " 'Cause I wish I had everything you hate."

"Would you like to have all these crummy feelings I have, too? Would you like to hate yourself, too?"

"If you were me, you would have to feel as bad as I do."

"If I was you I wouldn't be so stupid and feel so bad all the time."

A nurse walked in the room and caught the end of their conversation. "Are you two arguing to the last minute?" she asked with a frown. "You'll probably never see each other again, and this is no way to say goodbye."

"How do you know we'll never see each other again?" Lila protested.

The nurse bit her lip, then tried to explain, a bit embarrassed. "Well, hospital friendships are sometimes like summer camp friendships. You meet because you're in the same place, but then you have to leave." Her voice faded away.

Kessa and Lila looked at each other, both thinking the same thing. They lived in different neighborhoods, and they didn't have much in common, did they? Surgery had corrected Lila's club foot, but no simple operation could cure Kessa's anorexia nervosa.

Images flooded Kessa's head again, and she closed her eyes, remembering the day she'd been admitted.

Her face had been a blank. She'd be stuck in this building, and they were going to make her fat. She scanned the lobby, taking in the blandly colored walls, the scuffed terrazzo floor. No-nonsense and sterile. It was going to be very hard for her to fight there.

Three chattering women, wearing blue blazers with red carnations in their lapels, stood out like sore spots of color in the room. They politely answered visitors' questions, accepted flowers, surveyed their domain. Kessa turned away from them—she didn't want to smell any flowers—and looked at other people in the lobby. Many of them were as old as her grandparents, and some of them were sitting and talking to people who were much younger. One person, an elderly man in a wheelchair pushed by a nurse, passed Kessa. His head was tilted toward one side, and Kessa thought he looked embarrassed because he wasn't able to walk. I'm not ever getting in one of those things, she thought fiercely. Then a young woman, her face glowing, walked by with her husband, a newborn cradled lovingly in her arms. Did my parents look like that when I was born? Kessa wondered for an instant, then shook her head. Family—forget it. She'd show them. They might put her in the hospital, but she'd make them pay for it. They were forcing her here against her will, walking her quickly across the lobby as if they were afraid she might turn and run far away and never come back.

Kessa tried to pretend that she wasn't related to the man and woman walking so close to her. She worried instead how she could possibly fit in with the other patients she knew she'd have to meet in this hospital. It was more scary than anything she'd ever imagined.

They walked into the elevator, and Grace hit the button for the sixth floor.

"Dr. Gordon said we should just take you up to the nurses' station on six and get you settled in," she said, her voice all quavery. "Then we can go to the admissions office to take care of the paperwork."

Kessa remained silent, meanly glad that her mother sounded so nervous, so desperate for any sign of her daughter's approval, even though she was responsible for Kessa getting stuck here in the first place. Let her suffer, Kessa thought to herself over and over. She'd tried to say that out loud, but her mouth wouldn't open. She just stared as the buttons for each floor lit up until they reached six and the door opened and she stepped out and knew there was no escape.

Kessa didn't say a word to her parents, not even goodbye. They paused for a moment after seeing her to her room, waiting desperately for any acknowledgment, but Kessa sat woodenly on her bed and started tapping her thigh rhythmically. *Go home—go home—go home.*

Grace and Hal looked at each other, then turned to leave, their shoulders hunched in defeat.

After a few minutes, a nurse showed Kessa her room, pointing out a narrow closet and the chest with two drawers, the bathroom, the television's controls, and the meal menu that had been left on her table. When the nurse left, Kessa saw that the table next to the other bed was cluttered with magazines, makeup, and stuffed animals. So she had a roommate. Big deal. That girl just better leave her alone.

Kessa looked at the menu, but her eyes filled with tears and the lines all blurred together. She wanted to draw great big red *X*s through all three meal choices, then tear the menu up into a million pieces and watch them disappear. Instead, she kicked her suitcase into a corner and turned on the TV.

"Anyway," the nurse said softly, interrupting Kessa's reverie, "Kessa's parents are here to take her home, so say goodbye."

Hal and Grace walked in, smiling nervously, before Lila had a chance to say anything except, "'Bye, girl."

"Kessa, let's get going," Hal said.

Lila watched in silence, puzzled by their joyless glances.

Kessa quickly put on her coat, then gave Lila a ghost of a smile before she hurried out of the room.

Lila shook her head. When her parents came to get her, she'd be screaming with happiness. "Crazy," she said aloud. "Crazy skinny girl."

She shook her head again. "Poor Kessa."

Chapter
2

There were cleanly framed photographs of Andean mountain villages hanging on the walls of the waiting room in Sandy Sherman's office. Everything had been changed during Kessa's three-month stay in the hospital. The carpet was different, the walls had been repainted to a soft beige color, and the room was much larger. They must have knocked down a wall or something.

When an unfamiliar man came out into the waiting room and said hello, Kessa panicked, thinking for a minute that she might have stumbled into the wrong office.

"Is Dr. Sherman here?" she asked, trying to keep a tremor out of her voice.

"Yes," the man told her, smiling. "We've renovated the entire floor and the suite is much larger now. And there are three of us here, so you'll have lots of company in the waiting room. Sandy will be here in a minute."

Kessa tried to smile back and sat down, looking around at all the chairs. *Enough for an army,* she said to herself. *And I don't want to share this space with Sandy or anybody.*

She leaned back and closed her eyes. Memories of her last visit to this office, over three months before, flooded her head, unbidden. Back then, the walls had been light gray and the carpet had been darker gray and she had brought her five-foot four-inch frame down to seventy-two pounds. She remembered the increasingly worried look on the face of her pediatrician, Dr. Gordon. She remembered the anxiety of her parents—how they had warned, coaxed, pleaded, and threatened her. She remembered the sessions with Sandy. But nothing had kept the pounds on. She remembered the exact tone of his voice when he'd told her on the phone that she had to go to the hospital. He hadn't been angry, just calm, regretful almost.

"Kessa," he said. "I understand the idea is scary for you, but you're not being put in the hospital as a punishment. You're being put there to protect you, to make sure you won't die."

"But I don't want to go in. It sounds so final." She couldn't go to a hospital. She just couldn't! They'd stick tubes in her and all these thousands of calories would pour in and she'd swell up and get so fat she'd look like a blimp and just float away—

Why couldn't she keep seeing Sandy in his office? She thought of the room where they had their sessions. She saw it clearly in her head—the unoccupied lounge chair, the coffee table with the Kleenex box on it, the beechwood desk facing the wall, the bookcase, the three large windows behind his swivel chair. The more she imagined it, the more depressed she became. Her anger melted away and she felt this huge emptiness fill her body. She was an abandoned orphan. She would not be allowed in Sandy's office anymore. She would be stuck in some strange hospital room, where they'd be watching her all the time.

" . . . but it isn't final," Sandy was saying, "and it isn't a punishment."

"Please," she sobbed. "Please, I'm begging you. Don't put me in a hospital."

Kessa had no idea that, even after they hung up, her words continued to echo in Sandy's head. She would have been surprised to have seen him sitting quietly at his desk, anguished worry in his eyes, staring at the phone till the room darkened with the night.

Sandy Sherman walked into his office and saw Kessa, so deeply lost in thought that she didn't hear him enter. He studied her for a moment, noticing how still she was as she sat on his couch under one of his photographs of a mountain village, almost as if she were a stone statue in an overgrown and secret garden. Although the pounds she'd gained in the hospital had made her look less like a skeleton, Kessa was still gaunt. But it wasn't her thinness that brought a lump to Sandy's throat. It was her sadness.

He faked a cough. "Hi, Kessa. I just ran down for coffee."

Kessa stood up and nearly smiled in relief. At least Sandy hadn't changed. Same gray hair, same beard, even the same old sweater and knit tie. They went into his office —at least his room was still the same. Even the box of Kleenex on the glass coffee table looked untouched.

"Well, this is more like it," Sandy said as he sat down. "No more searching for privacy, an empty room to talk in. I'm certainly glad you're out of the hospital. How about you?"

"I thought it would be different."

"You thought you would be cured and happy?"

How did he know that's just what she'd been thinking? Kessa turned down the corners of her mouth and nodded vigorously. "When do I get to feel better?"

Sandy leaned back and waited.

"Why do I hate it when people tell me I look *so much better*?" She mimicked her mother's voice. "And when will I stop feeling so fat?" She smacked her thighs.

"You mean when will you stop feeling so bad?"

"These are fat thighs . . . everyone says so."

"You are five foot four and one hundred and two pounds. There's no room for any part of you to be fat at those proportions. What's really wrong?"

"I don't know how to live." Kessa surprised herself with the blunt honesty of that statement. Tears welled in her eyes, tears she didn't want her therapist to see.

After a minute's silence, Sandy said gently: "Then you'll need some help in learning how to live."

"You can't get help in learning how to live."

"I guess you don't believe that you can get help with anything. You think receiving help is bad stuff."

"I don't think anyone knows how to help anyone else— especially me."

"Is that why you've always been so careful?"

"What do you mean?" Kessa was stung. It sounded like he was accusing her of something.

"You've always been afraid to make any mistakes, as if a mistake would become a disaster. It's almost like you behave as if you were a war orphan, certain that there's no one around to protect you and any mistake could finish you off."

She looked up, surprised. "Yeah . . . it does feel like that."

"How come you feel like no one's there? You've got parents. They act like they care about you."

"They *do* care about me, as much as they can."

"Let's talk about how they fail."

"I don't want to do that."

"Why not?"

"It's not right."

"Not right to whom?"

"It's not right to pick on people who mean well."

"But you do that all the time."

She looked offended. "What do you mean?"

"You pick on *yourself* all the time. You hate the way you eat, no matter how much you eat or don't eat. You hate the way you look, no matter what your appearance is."

"That's different."

"Why?"

"I should know better."

"Better than who?"

Kessa had no answer.

"Better than everyone else in the world?"

She made a wry face but remained silent.

"It sounds silly when I say that, doesn't it?"

She nodded.

"Who do you trust to keep you safe?" Sandy asked.

"Me."

"But you don't do a very good job of it."

"What do you mean?"

"Look what this skinny business did to you. It nearly killed you and you still cling to it."

"You sound like Lila."

"Who's Lila?"

"A girl in the hospital. All she did was tell me how crazy I was."

"She sounds mean."

Kessa paused. "No, she wasn't really mean. She just said what was on her mind all the time. Like most people wouldn't say what they were thinking, but Lila didn't care."

Sandy remembered seeing the girl in the next bed when he'd visited Kessa in the hospital, but he'd never really thought about what their relationship might have been like. Maybe I should have, he thought. "What kind of things did she say?"

Kessa blushed and looked at her thighs. "She always wanted to know why I was so afraid to gain weight."

"What else?"

"She was critical of everything that I did."

"Sounds like a difficult roommate."

"She meant w— she was right. She thought I was nuts because no matter what happened, all I worried about was getting too fat. I guess I *am* nuts, after all."

"No, just looking for a simple solution."

"What's that supposed to mean?"

"It must be easier to control your weight than your life."

"But it's scary to control my weight . . . when I can."

"It sure seems a lot simpler to control what goes into your mouth and how many pounds the scale says than it is to feel safe among people."

"I manage fine with people," Kessa protested. "You ought to look at my old report cards." She began to mimic the comments teachers had written: " 'Works and plays well with others—excellent!' 'Cooperation—excellent!' 'A delight to have in the classroom!' "

"It sure sounds like you always managed people fine. It's too bad you weren't safe with them. There's a really big difference, Kessa. I bet you got to know everybody—and their personal problems—real well."

She nodded.

"I also bet no one has ever gotten to know *you* well."

"No one ever tried."

"I'm trying."

"This is different!"

"You always have an excuse."

"You're not my friend!"

"I'm a person who is helping you, and you hate to be helped."

Kessa stared down at the floor.

"Don't worry," he assured her. "You'll get better at it."

She looked up, puzzled.

"Receiving help is hard to learn how to do if you're used to thinking of it as a bad thing."

Chapter
3

Kessa walked home slowly through Central Park. She'd missed a whole season while she'd been in the hospital. While joggers had done their laps and children had chased balloons and couples had picnicked when the symphony had played free concerts under the stars, Kessa had been hooked up to an infusion pump that forced nutrition into her body so she wouldn't starve herself to death. She looked down at her body, hoping nobody would notice how fat she thought she was. *Thirty-three pounds into my veins! Now everyone can see what a pig they made me with that stupid calorie pump.*

Kessa shuddered as she remembered her first week in the hospital. Her weight had dropped to sixty-nine pounds. Her body was starting to fall apart—her liver, kidneys, and heart were all functioning abnormally—so a surgeon and his team made an incision in her chest and placed a narrow catheter into her jugular vein. This tube went with her everywhere. It was like a part of her, a *piece* of her that she didn't want but couldn't get rid of. It forced two thousand calories a day into her body. Kessa thought obsessively about that pump. She hated it. Its line was taped to her shoulder from its entry site just below the right side of her collarbone, and it was attached to the blue rectangular box affixed to a chrome pole on wheels. The I-VAC logo gleamed at her. Above it was the one-inch-square button with the picture of an upraised hand, which blinked on and off to indicate that the fluid was flowing. The steel casing was only a little over a foot in height, six inches deep and three wide. It reminded her of a taxi meter, except this small window here indicated the number of drops per minute—how fat she was getting, by the minute.

And that medical scale they made her stand on was worse. It never lied. It was tangible proof of how fat she was getting. Sometimes it seemed to Kessa that the infusion pump and the scale weren't inanimate objects anymore. They were real and alive and talking to each other, using her body like a telephone. . . . And she remembered the day she'd fought with Sherman over the infusion pump. He'd been ten minutes late and hurried in, looking preoccupied. She thought he'd forgotten all about her.

"I gained three pounds this week!" Kessa shouted angrily.

Sandy stopped so quickly he nearly ran into the foot of her bed. He looked from her face to the infusion pump as though it was his colleague and then back to her. "That's exactly what you were supposed to gain."

"But I didn't eat anything! What will happen when I start to eat? Don't you see? Now I'll never be able to eat anything!"

"If you gain more than three pounds in one week, we'll turn the pump down." Sandy tried to keep the exasperation out of his voice. Sometimes Kessa's distortion was so frustrating he found it hard to keep himself from saying something he knew he'd regret.

"And what am I supposed to do in the meantime?" Kessa was still furious.

"We're supposed to work on your perspective. The three pounds you're shouting so much about has brought your weight up to seventy-five pounds. For a five-foot four-inch person, seventy-five pounds is about thirty-five pounds underweight."

Her face tightened and Sandy braced himself for more screams of protest. Instead, Kessa leaned back against her pillow and started to cry.

"You can't make me gain thirty-five pounds. I can't handle that. I'll be fatter than I ever wanted to be."

"Kessa," Sandy tried to reassure her. "It's not important for you to be an 'average' weight. But you need to become a minimal menstrual weight. That would be around a hundred and one pounds."

"Why do I have to be a hundred and one?" She sounded slightly relieved.

Sandy ventured a sympathetic smile. "Because at a hundred and one you'll be at a minimum appropriate weight and you'll have done something else that's important. You'll be tolerating a weight in three digits. I didn't just pull a hundred and one out of thin air. There's something deliberate about it—it's two numbers above ninty-nine."

Kessa bit her lip to hold back more tears. That wasn't what she wanted to hear. "If you know about numbers being important to me, then why do you want me to weigh a weight that makes me nervous?"

Sandy looked at her desperate face. "Kessa, numbers have become more important to you than people. It's numbers and an emaciated or 'special' appearance that comfort you most, right?"

She nodded slowly, not meeting his gaze.

"We have two objectives in hospitalizing you," he continued. "The first is to change your weight and appearance. The second is to help you make the leap from only trusting things, procedures, and numbers to keep you safe. We want you to learn how to trust people to keep you safe, to comfort you and make you feel secure."

"But people have never made me feel safe! That's just never been true! And now I'm stuck here. I'm stuck on this machine that's making me fat—no, it's taking away what's more important to me than anything, my control over my weight—and you want me to feel safe and comforted? Fat chance! How the hell are you going to do that, Dr. Know-It-All Sherman?" Kessa turned her head away, then tried to sigh. The outburst had taken most of her energy.

Sandy watched her for a minute, then said, "You may not think so today, and today you're right. It will take time for it to happen."

Kessa's face tightened. "Oh yeah? How much time? How long am I going to be stuck here?"

"Until you're able to maintain your goal weight by eating and not by having this machine attached to you."

"That will take forever." Kessa's voice trailed off.

"No it won't. It would take forever if we had to wait for you to decide to eat and to gain by yourself. Right now your eating and gaining are not related. For the first time since you got sick, your eating will not affect your weight. It does not represent control."

Kessa looked straight at Sandy, partly angry, partly bewildered. "Then I have no control."

"That's true."

"So how am I going to feel safe without any control?"

"For a while you won't feel safe."

Kessa crossed her arms and pouted.

Sandy stood up. "I guess you'll learn to control something

else if you can't control your weight," he said as he left the room, pulling the door shut behind him.

Kessa turned on her side and felt the plastic line connecting her to the pump and its fattening fluid brush across her shoulder. Automatically, she slowed her movements to prevent the line from pulling at its entry site on her chest. She felt extra fat. Her legs beneath the covers already looked enormous. She jerked the covers off and pulled her nightgown up to see if her bare legs looked thinner than they did covered. The longer she stared at them, the thicker they appeared. She pressed her legs harder against the mattress, which caused them to spread slightly, then punched each thigh with her fist and flung herself down hard on her back. Only as her head hit the pillow did she have a twinge of fear about jerking the intravenous line.

She stared at the blue pump again, musing over how much it had become a part of her. It really was almost like a person. "Well, at least you're the one who's making me gain weight, not me." She pulled the plug out of its wall socket at the head of her bed and wound the cord around the hook provided for it, switching it to battery operation to prevent that annoying beeping sound it made when unplugged, and wheeled it to the bathroom. As she closed the bathroom door behind her, she addressed the machine once more:

"It's a good thing the bathroom is built for the two of us."

Kessa heard shouts and screams of laughter, and she realized she'd walked nearly all the way across the park in a total daze. Dumb me, she said to herself. I bet I even have fat cells clogging my brain. She looked over at a group of teenagers playing catch with a tattered hat, then decided to sit on a large rock and watch them for a while. Why was it so easy for them to laugh as if they didn't have a care in the world? Kessa was jealous. She didn't know how to fit in. Sandy was right. She could "manage" everyone, but that made her life an awfully lonely one. And it was all because she was too fat.

She looked more closely at the girls playing catch. They all seemed to be about her age, and they were all fatter than she was. And one of them even looked familiar too. Lila! It *was* Lila, her roommate from the hospital. Lila looked so happy, and they'd taken the cast off her foot. The operation must have been a success. Lila was still limping, but she was laughing so much, her foot couldn't still be hurting. Or maybe she was so glad to be out of the hospital that she didn't notice any pain. Kessa's admiration for Lila made her forget how mad she'd been at the girl who was on her case from the minute she realized Kessa was too crazy to eat even when she was starving to death. And she never let up.

Lila sensed that someone was looking at her and glanced up. Kessa. Sitting, hunched up, all alone on a rock. Crazy skinny Kessa.

Lila squinted, trying to decide if she should acknowledge that mixed-up rich kid from the hospital. Well, even if Kessa lived in a fancy apartment building on Central Park West, they could still share the same park.

"Hey, Kessa!" she shouted without even thinking. Even if that white girl was rich and stuck-up, she was still poor, crazy, lonely Kessa.

Kessa pretended to be surprised.

"Lila!"

Lila's friends looked surprised as she greeted this stranger like a long-lost friend.

She turned to them. "That's the kid from the hospital I told you about."

As they nodded knowingly to each other, Kessa tensed.

The kid from the hospital. Lila and Kessa stopped at arm's length, trying to decide how to greet each other. Lila stuck out her hand, and Kessa took it.

Lila smiled. "Hey, you look good!"

"Thanks."

"I really didn't know if you could do it."

"Do what?"

"Keep lookin' okay."

Kessa blushed deeply. It was true she didn't want to "keep lookin' okay," but that was something she kept to herself. Lila talking about it in front of her friends was totally humiliating. They'd all stare at her like she was crazy, and think she was fat. It was almost as if Lila was standing on top of that rock and announcing to the world that Kessa had anorexia, that her most intense struggles and pain were there to be mocked.

"Yeah, no big deal. Well, I'll see you around." Kessa had to get out of there. She waved Lila off, glanced at the group, and hurried quickly away.

What did I say? Lila asked herself. *I didn't mean to make her split. That girl must be better if she wasn't back in the hospital, but she was still pretty skinny. Poor Kessa.*

Lila shook her head and limped back to her friends.

Kessa walked into her apartment house lobby. It was the domain of Charles, the elevator operator, who had worked there for thirty years and maintained a proprietary attitude toward the building and its tenants. To him, everyone was family, and he was the reigning grandfather.

"Well, out for a stroll, Miss Dietrich?"

She nodded, trying to smile.

"You're looking better than you did last spring." He meant it as a compliment, but she bristled at the remark.

Charles noticed her frown and cleared his throat. "Well, I hope you're feeling all right," he said without looking at her. He brought the elevator to the ninth floor in silence.

Chapter
4

Kessa quietly let herself in. Her family was lucky to have such a nice large apartment. There were three hallways connecting the living room-dining room-kitchen area with the three bedrooms. There was even a maid's bedroom off the kitchen, but they used it as a laundry room. All the rooms were oversized and featured high beamed ceilings. The interior walls actually had bricks at their center and thick plaster on the outside surfaces. This made every room in the apartment nearly soundproof from the next. Even shouting didn't guarantee that one would be heard throughout the apartment, as Kessa and her parents knew all too well.

Grace Dietrich was straightening up the pots in the cupboard when she heard her daughter in the hallway. She stopped automatically and hurried out of the kitchen. Being in the kitchen with her daughter still made her nervous.

"Hi, Mom," Kessa said.

"Hello, dear." Her voice was quavery.

"Weren't you just in the kitchen?"

"Yes, but I'm finished now. Do you need anything there?"

Kessa was becoming annoyed, but she didn't know why. "No! I don't need anything there! I just wanted to know where you were. We've got a big apartment, and I wanted to tell you about Lila . . . oh, forget it!"

"If you're going to be so volatile, it's going to ruin the evening for Daddy as well."

"I'm sorry I'm going to be ruining your evening. I'm sorry to be in charge of your evening anyway!" Kessa ran down the hall and slammed the door of her bedroom.

Grace slowly walked over to her daughter's room, pangs of guilt shooting through her, though she had no idea what offense she'd committed to get Kessa so upset. She knocked softly.

"Why don't you open the door? Then you can tell me about Lila. Wasn't she the girl who was your roommate in the hospital?"

"I don't think I want to talk about it anymore. Everything we ever talk about is either food or the hospital." Kessa started sobbing.

Grace leaned her head against her daughter's door. *I'm a failure*, she thought. *I've created a monster*. She remembered a phone call soon after Kessa's hospital admission.

"How are you doing, dear?" Grace had asked.

"I don't see how you think that this will help me." Kessa couldn't stand hearing such deference in her mother's voice. It was an open invitation for rage.

Grace remained silent, struggling with her guilt and anger.

"I'm sure when you become adjusted to the hospital you'll be more positive about it, Francesca."

"You're wasting your time, Mother," Kessa shouted into the phone.

"Francesca, I didn't call you to argue about whether you're going to stay in the hospital or not."

"Well, that's all I want to talk about." She was still shouting.

"I'll call you tommorrow, then—"

Kessa slammed down the receiver.

Grace stood up straight. *I've got to keep trying,* she told herself. *I've got to learn to talk to my daughter.* "Kessa!" This was the first time Grace used the nickname Francesca had given herself. "Why don't you just open the door and we'll talk."

"Okay."

"Kessa . . ." she began awkwardly, realizing how wrong she'd been by ignoring her daughter's preference for a name. "I don't want us to be upset every time we talk to each other. Why don't you tell me what's the matter."

"I'm just upset because everybody deals with me the same way they did before I went to the hospital. All everyone does is look at me through the corner of their eyes when I eat or when I go to the bathroom. Sometimes I think you're all standing outside the bathroom door to see if I'm barfing or something. You make me paranoid in my own home. And I'm mad at all of you for wanting me to be fat!"

Grace was shocked by Kessa's outburst. She thought of the skeleton that her daughter had become prior to hospitalization. Kessa was still thinner than normal, so how could she be calling herself fat?

"We don't want you to be fat, Kessa. We just want you to be healthy."

"Fat or healthy—it's the same thing! All you care about is my weight! When you tell me I look good, I get mad. . . . I get furious! It's like you won!"

"What do you mean, I won?" That was it. The last straw.

Grace simply could not take any more accusations from her daughter. She forgot her vow to try and talk to Kessa, understand her illness. "Is this whole horrible ordeal we're still going through a contest? And if you win, what does that mean? Does it mean you'll look like a skeleton forever? Or do you die, so you know you're the winner forever. But you're not around to celebrate your victory, are you?" Grace barely paused for breath. So much anger, so much fear, had been bottled inside for too long. "Is this whole thing some sort of sick rebellion? If it is, then why don't you try shoplifting, or have an abortion like your sister, or smoke pot in the bathroom. As a rebellion, or as some sick way to prove your independence from your father and me, I think it's pathetic!"

Now it was Grace's turn to slam the door.

Kessa wished she were emaciated again. She was in control then. They were afraid of her then. She sat down on her rocking chair and stared at her thighs, which spread naturally from the pressure of the hard wooden seat. Thin to her parents, they seemed terrifyingly fat to her. She was getting fat. Not rebellious. Kessa could hardly think of herself that way. It was her sister, Suzanna, who was rebellious—Suzanna who ran off to get birth control; Suzanna who got pregnant anyway. Kessa didn't even have any romantic interest in boys, and certainly had no desire for sex. It was her sister who left the family to live on a cooperative farm in California. How could Kessa's mother accuse her of what was unthinkable?

The phone rang in Kessa's hospital room. She jerked her head automatically to the left but stopped her hand just before it reached the receiver. Instead, she stared at the

phone. None of her school friends had called. Her grandmother had phoned only two days ago. It was probably just
her mother. At the fifth ring, she decided to pick up.

"Hello," she said sullenly.

"H'ya, Francesca?"

Kessa was startled. "Suzanna?"

"How's my kid sister?"

"It's really you!"

"It is, and get used to it. I'll be here for three weeks."

"Great. Are you going to visit me?"

Suzanna bit her lip. Her sister's voice sounded younger.
The question she'd just asked had a depressing desperation.
"I'll be up tomorrow. Will they let me come in the
morning?"

Kessa paused for a moment. No one had asked her that
question. "Oh sure. I see visitors here, um, from ten in the
morning on."

"Then I'll be there at ten."

" 'Bye."

" 'Bye, Francesca."

Kessa could feel her initial enthusiasm slipping away as
the conversation ended. Suzanna didn't even know her name
was Kessa, not Francesca. Everyone knew that but her own
family.

She lay there in bed staring at the silent phone, wondering
what it would be like to see her sister. Even thinking about
Suzanna made her tense, making her want to lose more
weight. She was just getting too fat. She looked around her
room. The room was her whole world. This antiseptic, heart-
less room. *I have no life outside of this place,* she thought,
feeling completely inferior and defective. *Nobody knows
me. I'm simply the patient in 455B. I'm nobody.*

Panic made her sit up quickly. She looked at her hospital

ID bracelet, turning the plastic around to see the white
paper with the large blue type underneath its smooth plastic
sleeve. FRANCESCA LOUISE DIETRICH, it read.

She reached over to the bed table and picked up a ball-
point pen. Over *Francesca* she wrote *Kessa* once, then again,
and then for the third time until all the letters were unread-
able. "I'm Kessa," she shouted as she threw the pen across
the room. "Kes-sa, Kes-sa, Kes-sa!" Her voice dissolved into
sobs. She tried to tear the ID bracelet off, but the plastic was
too tough, so she turned the band around so the letters were
hidden. At least Lila was in therapy and she was alone.

Kessa leaned back against the pillows and rolled her head
rhythmically from right to left. She thought about how the
sound of her own voice seemed so strange to her, as if it were
someone else's. Maybe it *was* someone else's. When she
spoke to her family, she felt like a robot. She heard the
sound of her voice, but it felt like it wasn't even connected to
her own body. It came from someplace very far away. And it
was always the worst with her family.

"Soon they'll forget me. They'll have to," Kessa said to
the sterile walls. "I'm so boring, I'm so nothing. Nobody
could want me for a daughter, a sister, a friend. . . . anything. Nobody wants a nothing. I'm ugly, boring, dumb,
ugly, ugly, ugly." She repeated the word aloud until it was a
chant and the sound of it filled her head. "Ug—*ly*, ug—*ly*,
ug—*ly*, ug—"

Kessa didn't realize she was crying again until she started
hiccuping. She reached for the box of tissues and wiped her
face, but the tears kept flowing. What did it matter? Kessa
realized she was terrified that soon she wouldn't know what
anything meant. Would that mean she was insane? *Is this
what it feels like to be nuts?* Until now, she had viewed the
hospital as the enemy. Now it looked like an authoritative
condemnation of her state of mind. *I'm here because I'm*

crazy, she said to herself. *They all think I'm crazy. I don't belong anywhere anymore.* An inescapable feeling of fearful loneliness intensified as she lay there. *I'll never feel connected to anyone else.* She looked up at the IV bottle, followed the plastic tubing down through the blue I-VAC pump and into the bandage on the left side of her chest. "This machine is my only friend," she told the sterile walls of her room. "It feeds me. It's hooked right into my bloodstream. It doesn't make fun of me. It's always there." Her voice became a sob. "Damn you, Suzanna! Why do you always make me feel so inferior? I'm never interesting next to you. I can't help it if I didn't need a diaphragm when I turned sixteen. I can't help it if I don't want to live on a cooperative in California. Here I am—Harold Dietrich's less interesting daughter! Francesca Louise Dietrich, also known as Kessa, the skinny kid everybody's mad at."

Kessa blew her nose loudly just as an aide walked in with dinner. Kessa turned on her side, but the aide saw the swollen, tear-stained eyes anyway.

"Are you all right, honey?"

Her sympathetic inquiry made Kessa embarrassed. She rolled back over, licking away the tears that still fell to the corners of her mouth.

"Heah—yeah, thanks. Don't worry, I'm okay."

"Do you want me to call a nurse? Does something hurt?"

"No, everything's okay. Really. Thanks for asking." Kessa forced a smile.

The aide smiled back and placed Kessa's dinner on her bed tray. Kessa ignored it. Instead, she reached for the telephone to call Sherman. She looked at her watch while dialing. Six o'clock. She hoped he was still at the office.

"Hello?"

"Sandy, is that you?"

"Yes it's me. What is it, Kessa?"

"I'm freaking out. I don't know what's going on. Do you know who I am?"

He paused for a moment to let those three sentences register. Sometimes Kessa knocked him out.

"Yes, Kessa," he said in a slow, even voice. "I know who you are. You don't sound strange to me. You do sound confused and scared. But you sound like *you* to me."

"I just hate being who I am! Why do I have to be such a crazy person? Why does my head spin all the time? I always think twenty thoughts at once. I can never stop. Will I always be like this? Will I ever feel different? Because if I'll never feel different, why should I gain weight? Why should I *try* to do anything?

Her panic and despair sent Sandy's mind racing for a helpful answer.

"Kessa, has something happened in the hospital? Has your weight changed too quickly for you?"

"No. Nothing's happened at all. I was just sitting here and suddenly everything started to feel worse and worse!"

"Did anyone call?"

"No. Yes. Wait a minute. Suzanna, my sister, called."

"What did she say?"

"Nothing. She just said she would visit me tomorrow."

"How do you feel about her coming?"

"Oh c'mon, *Dr*. Sherman, I feel fine about . . ."

He could hear her sigh. "Kessa, maybe it doesn't feel as good as it's supposed to when your sister calls or visits you."

"Maybe not. Is that what this is all about?"

"Partly. Do you want to tell me how Suzanna makes you feel?"

"Boring." That word just slipped out before she even realized it. Kessa had to snicker, she was so surprised by the admission. "I don't know why I said that."

"That's good."

"What do you mean, that's good?"

Sandy relaxed a little, feeling a little more attuned to her mood.

"Kessa, it's good because it's unrehearsed talk."

"What does that mean?"

"It means that you never had the thought that your sister makes you feel boring until you said it. When you say something that you never even thought about before, it means you're breaking new ground, you're developing new insights about yourself. When that happens, you become surprised or guilty, even disappointed, but in a moment it turns to relief. You feel more whole."

"Is that good?"

"How do you feel now compared with the way you felt before you called?"

"Better. But maybe it's —"

"It's what?"

"Maybe it's . . . you."

Sandy was glad she couldn't see him blush. "Well, I'm surely part of the process."

Kessa sensed his embarrassment and dropped it, thinking that maybe she was too much of a burden for him.

"Dr. Sherman . . . is it wrong for me to . . ."

"What, Kessa?"

"To feel good just because I talk to you? Oh, I know that what we say is important. I know that you always talk about the *work* that we do. I mean, am I allowed to feel better no matter what we say? Even if we fight? It doesn't always. As a matter of fact, sometimes I feel worse when we talk and I don't even know why. Do *you* know what I mean?"

"Kessa, it would be unrealistic to treat 'our work' as textbook learning. Feelings are part of what we do."

"Yeah, but that's weird. And confusing. I mean, you're not my mother or my father. You're my therapist—

whatever that is. I only see you when I have an appointment with you. That's not real."

"One person helping another is real. I don't have to be your parent in order to help you."

"That sounds okay, but I don't know where to put it. I never talked about myself like this to anybody."

"How does it leave you feeling?"

"It leaves me feeling vulnerable. It also leaves me feeling possessive. I don't like the idea that you talk to other people like you talk to me. It makes me jealous."

"Kessa, do you feel angry because you don't have a parent, or a person all to yourself?"

"*Shit!*" The dam broke. "My sister Suzanna *still has* my mother to herself. She always had her. I could never break into their private thing, their secret talk! No matter how nice my mother is to me, I'll never be as much a part of her as my sister. I mean, I think I'm the better daughter. I worry about my mother. I'm thoughtful about her. I even feel like I take care of her in some strange way. It's just that Suzanna always got something from her I can't. She *feels* something from her that I can't. You know, the craziest thing is that I think I get from you what my sister gets from my mother." She paused for half a minute, then continued in a very low voice. "You know, a couple of times I almost called you Mom." She started to cry. "Why, Sandy? You're not my mother!"

"Every family has its own system. All members get some things they want out of it but feel they're missing others. We don't have to get all the kinds of satisfaction we need from our families alone. It's easier if we can get the important ones, but whatever is missing in our family relationships can be gotten elsewhere as we grow up."

"Is that why I want to call you Mom?"

"Probably."

"And sometimes I get mad at you—madder than I have a right to be."

"I think you get as mad at me as you need to be. We can work arguments out and get past them."

"But I get confused again. Who are you to me?"

"The person helping you with yourself."

"But there's no such thing! I mean, are you a parent to me—and how could you be? I can only see you at special times, and my parents pay you anyway. How could one person be paid to help another?"

The mention of payment reminded Sandy of the constant conflict he felt about this ethical dilemma. Kessa was right to pose such a question.

"Kessa, therapy isn't part of our family life and it isn't part of our social life. It's a self-conscious relationship that helps us grow. It's carefully structured with appointments and time limits and offers a reliability and certainty that family and friendships may not, but it is also restricted in a way that those relationships aren't."

"Does that mean that it's fake?"

"No . . . just careful."

"If I care about you . . ."

"Yes?"

"I don't know. I mean . . . do you ever care about me?"

"Have you ever had teachers who cared about you, who liked you and wanted good things for your future?"

"Yes. I think so. But I never cared about them as much . . ."

"Then I'll have to be even more careful with you than they were."

"So is this real?"

"Could you be fooled?"

"I don't think so." Kessa almost smiled.

"Then it's real. I'll see you tomorrow at eight-thirty in the morning, Kessa."

" 'Bye."

They hung up. Kessa heaved a huge sigh. She had wanted to tell him that she wished that he didn't have any other patients, that when she came out of the hospital she didn't want to meet the other people he saw in his office. She knew that he had a family, but at least she didn't have to see them—his wife and two children. As long as she didn't see them, they really didn't exist. She didn't feel so separated from the rest of the world anymore. Maybe someday all of this would go away and leave her in peace.

She sat for a long time in the chair, rocking gently, wishing she were thinner. Somehow that would make all of this turmoil vanish.

Chapter
5

Grace sat alone at the work counter in her kitchen, feeling as if she had only recently recaptured this room and all it symbolized from her daughter. She paid no attention to the celery she was idly chopping just to keep her fingers busy. She wished she were at the beach, because Kessa made her think of waves—endlessly rolling waves of anger and guilt. The waves fluctuated but they never went away, kept interminably breaking. Was the girl helplessly sick or had she devised this illness as some sort of all-encompassing, sinister plot against her mother? Had the Dietrichs focused that much upon their older son and daughter at the expense of the youngest? Had Grace really neglected this once charming girl, now turned tyrant?

Grace stopped chopping. In her memory, she heard a phone ring.

"Hello, Francesca?"

"Oh hi, Mom."

"Did you sister call you today?"

"Yeah."

"Well, you don't sound enthusiastic. Wasn't she nice to you on the phone?"

"Yes, Mom, she was nice to me on the phone. It's just very complicated. I don't feel that great when I talk to her." *And*, she wanted to add, *whenever I talk to you I always feel fatter.*

"I just don't understand that. She came all the way from California to—"

"Mom, you're not going to tell me that she came all the way from California just to see me, are you?"

"No. It's just that I like to see my daughters getting along with each other better than this sounds."

"How does it sound when you talk to Suzanna? Does *she* sound all bubbly about me?"

"Perhaps I should call you later, when you're not so upset, Francesca." Why did this daughter make every simple statement so complicated? Grace just couldn't cope. They hadn't been on the phone for more than a minute and she already wanted to hang up.

Grace had no idea that her conversation created the familiar, searing stabs of rejection in Kessa. She was siding with Suzanna, as usual. It didn't matter what Kessa felt.

"I don't see why you have to hang up just because I sound upset to you. We could keep talking until things become agreeable."

"I'm afraid I don't know at this point what you really want from me," Grace said.

"I don't know what I really want from you, Mother, but I can tell I'm not getting it now. Okay, you're right. I'll talk to you later."

The phone clicked off before Grace had a chance to say anything.

She looked at the chopped celery, then put the knife down

on the counter, absentmindedly wiping her hands as she did so. She poured a cup of coffee and sat down near the window, sipping the hot black liquid and brooding. Kessa was still a mystery to her. Suzanna had been so brazen, so intimidating—it had been so much easier to give in to her precociously outrageous demands.

Had Kessa always been listening to them—and they'd never listened to her?

Grace thought of the months of coaxing, the fears, the inexorable landslide to Kessa's hospitalization: the final blow condemning her as a mother. And what was most ironic was that it took Suzanna's visit from California to make her see how much of a failure she truly was.

Suzanna had arrived from San Francisco, and as soon as her father came home from work, the two of them were at each other's throats . . .

"I just can't understand why," Harold had said. "I mean, why Francesca? Of all the children for this to happen to—"

"You mean," Suzanna cut in, "if there was any justice, it would have happened to me."

Here we go again, Grace had thought to herself—*and so soon.*

The argument had raged until Hal stormed out of the living room.

"Well, it looks like I'm home," Suzanna had said.

Grace was silent.

"Aren't you going to say anything?"

"I was just thinking, Suzanna. About Francesca, not about you. We started out talking about her, but we ended up fighting about you."

"That's the story of my life."

"It's the story of your sister's life, too. Maybe that's what's wrong."

*   *   *

After a dinner eaten in silence, Harold tried to apologize. "Suzanna, you just got back from California. I'm feeling a lot older than when you left. I would like us to stop arguing. We had to put your sister in the hospital because she's obsessed with the idea of getting fat, and she's driving us and herself nuts. You're nice and healthy and I don't want to fight with you, okay?"

But that wasn't okay. "See, even that doesn't sound like a compliment. I'm okay only if my sister's crazy. I'm only successful if Francesca's out of the way. Thanks a whole lot."

They both looked at Grace, who had always played referee during their arguments.

"If you two want to go at each other, it's all right with me. I'm no longer the mediator. I think you'll have to figure out how to work out your relationship without my help."

A direct confrontation was too much for Suzanna, so she changed the subject.

"Why *is* Francesca in the hospital?"

"So they can keep her alive," Harold answered matter-of-factly.

"What do you mean?"

"Francesca wasn't eating enough to keep herself going," Grace said. "She weighed about sixty-nine pounds when we had her admitted."

Suzanna was shocked. She had never really worried about her little sister, never really thought about what made her tick. After all, their father had always spoken of her as "the best little girl in the world."

"Does she still look like that? I mean, when we go to the hospital, is that what we'll see?"

"No." Harold made an ineffectual gesture. "Don't look so worried. She's gained ten pounds."

"Is she eating better?"

"We don't think so."

"Then how is she gaining weight?"

"They put a tube in her jugular vein and it pumps two thousand calories a day into her body."

Suzanna went pale. "How disgusting! Why doesn't she just eat?"

Harold smiled at her. "That's a very good question. Nobody seems to have the answer."

"That's crazy. I'll talk to her."

"It won't be so easy. She's not like she was."

Suzanna looked at her father, then turned toward her mother. They both looked at her patiently, as if waiting for her to comprehend the incomprehensible. The silence only lasted a few seconds, but it seemed like eternity passed by.

"You both act like she's lost her mind or something, like she's crazy!"

Silence became oppressive. Harold raised his eyebrows in acknowledgment and nodded.

Suzanna's outrage dissipated and tears filled her eyes. Was her sister really crazy? "You know, I was always jealous of Francesca," she said in a low voice. "Everything she did was always right. Everything I did was always wrong. I always figured I'd go through life screwing up and she would succeed every step of the way. A lot of times I thought about how much I hated her, how I wished she'd stop getting straight A's and all those comments about how great she was on her report cards." She stopped to blow her nose.

"Now it's like she's dead. Now she sounds like some kind of creature—not even a real person anymore. She's probably disgusting to look at and" —her voice rose— "crazy. I don't want her to be crazy! I'd rather be jealous of her. I miss my perfect little sister!"

She ran over to Grace and buried her head on her

mother's shoulder, sobbing wildly. Grace patted her on the back, the way she had when Suzanna was young. Harold sat woodenly, his hands clenched tightly together, and stared at the floor. There was nothing to say.

The next morning was rainy and dismal, still so gloomy at nearly ten that the streetlights were still on. The weather seemed to match their moods as Suzanna and her parents slammed their car doors shut in the hospital parking lot and snapped open their umbrellas.

"It feels like we're going to a funeral," Suzanna said.

Grace turned toward her. Her daughter seemed younger today, small and very scared. She remembered how Suzanna always tried to disguise any fears by being brazen or angry or even remaining silent. Grace couldn't remember the last time she'd heard any fear in Suzanna's voice. Today it was there.

"It's more frustrating than frightening," she said gently.

Grace led the way, through the lobby, up to the sixth floor past the nurses' station. She knew just which door was Kessa's. Harold felt self-conscious, hoping no one he knew would see him with the skeleton his daughter had become. As he approached her room, the tenderness of the day before rapidly dissipated into nervous frustration.

Grace came in first, followed by Suzanna and Harold. Kessa looked up, her face blank.

Suzanna tried to hide a wave of panic. This bedridden creature couldn't be her sister. She forced a smile, holding back tears of shock and shame, and gave Kessa a quick hug.

"How're you doin', kid?" Suzanna asked softly, her voice husky with emotion.

Kessa shrugged. "I'm stuck here, bored and getting fat."

"It looks like you've got a long way to go to get fat, kid."

Kessa looked at the sheets and started tapping her thigh rhythmically. Suzanna realized she was facing a stranger: She saw an emaciated figure, the outline of the skeletal arms, the pelvic bones protruding through the pajamas, the ribcage appearing like so many stripes down to the first button on her top. Her hair was thinner than Suzanna remembered it.

Kessa felt the weight of her sister's gaze and wanted to yell at her to stop. But it was easier to remain silent and pretend that she wasn't there, that she was very far away.

"Francesca, did they tell you how long you have to be here?"

"What?" Kessa looked up blankly. *Kessa*, she said vehemently to herself, *my name is Kessa. Francesca doesn't exist anymore.*

Suzanna repeated the question, wanting to pretend her sister was in the hospital only until some physical "condition" beyond her control would be cleared up by the doctors, like appendicitis or something. Kessa appreciated the gesture, but it made her feel even more ashamed. So she got mad.

"Haven't you heard? I'm going to be here till hell freezes over! Until I'm a 'good' girl again."

For the first time in her life, Suzanna was thoroughly intimidated by her little sister. This frightening-looking skeleton made her feel completely helpless. "I guess you're in a bad mood today, huh?"

"I don't know what Mom and Dad think this is going to do for me. If they want me to gain weight, I don't see why they don't just take me home and let me gain the weight there."

Her logic stopped Suzanna. Grace and Harold, who now stood together near the door, felt their habitual pangs of guilt and self-reproach. Suzanna looked at her sister's emaciated limbs and started to feel her usual confidence coming back. Confrontations were easy for her. If her sick little sister was going to provoke one, then she'd get what she asked for.

"Yeah, sis, I'm sorry to have to say this, but you must be crazy," Suzanna said sarcastically. She didn't mean to sound harsh, but she had absolutely no idea what to say. "If you think that it's all right to look like this and if this is how you looked when they brought you in here, *they* would be nuts to bring you home like this."

Kessa blanched and stared down at the sheets again, picking nervously at them.

Grace tried to defend her. "Suzanna, your sister is not crazy. She's just stuck on the issue of weight."

"She doesn't look just a little stuck to me."

"We didn't come here to argue about or fight with Francesca," Harold interjected. "Let's try to keep this pleasant."

"*She* should get over whatever she *has* so we wouldn't be here in the first place, Daddy."

"Francesca," Harold said in his most authoritative tone, "do you think you're making progress since you've been here?"

Her father's words stung as sharply as a severe insult. Kessa refused to look up or acknowledge the question in any way. She remained silent for what seemed like ages, though it was only a few minutes, and kept picking at the sheets until they left her alone.

As the elevator took them down, Harold exploded. "Grace, that's the worst I've ever seen her. Are you sure this is the best place for her?"

"I'm not sure of anything, Harold."

"Well, how are we supposed to know if she's getting better? Or when she'll start to get better?"

"It takes a long time. Please don't ask me how long. I just don't know."

Suzanna stood in silence, trying to comprehend the metamorphosis of Francesca. The wooden figure sitting in that bed was not her little sister.

Chapter
6

Kessa took her usual seat on the couch in Sherman's office, opposite the eight-foot windows, which seemed to dwarf her against the cityscape beyond. Today, the pearl-gray autumn sky held the threat of an early snow. Kessa felt as drab as the weather.

"Do you remember when I called you after Suzanna's first visit to the hospital and said how my family looked weird and sounded weird when they talked to me?"

"Was that when I suggested family therapy?"

"Yeah." Kessa focused on the leaden sky, remembering.

Kessa sat like a stone statue in bed, tears coursing down her woebegone face and staining the sheets. A nurse who was new to the floor peered in to check on her patients, saw the distraught girl, and hurried in, concern wrinkling her brow.

"Is there anything you need, honey?"

Kessa shook her head. "Thank you for asking." The standard reply of a child who wants to please.

"I could sit with you for a while if you like."

"No thanks. I'll be all right. It's just a passing mood."
She feigned a smile and wiped her eyes until the nurse left.

Kessa got up slowly and walked over to the window,
gazing down six floors to the street leading to the hospital's
front entrance. She watched the arriving and departing cars
with their cargo of people, watched the pedestrians crossing
to the parking lot. Each of them must have a place in life,
she thought—a job, a family, friends, things to do. She was
not a part of any of that. She belonged nowhere. Her
confinement in this hospital room was an official verification
that she did not belong out there with everyone else. No one
liked the way she looked. Everyone was angry at what made
her happy and safe. She knew she was a freak because
everyone hated what she needed: the special thinness, the
control.

Will I always be an outcast? she wondered as she eased
her way back into bed and picked up the phone. Dr. Sherman answered.

"Hello, Sandy."

"Kessa?"

"Yeah."

"What is it? What's the matter?"

"I'm lousy again."

"What do you mean?"

"I'm hating my life again. Can you do anything for me?"

"No miracles. But I'll listen for a while if you'll talk."

"*They were here!*" Her voice rose to a scream. "They
came here to see me. All they did was make me feel like a
miserable failure! Why the hell did they come? I didn't ask
them to come. I wish that they'd never come again, and I bet
they do too. Why is it that no matter how much I hate them,
in the end I always think that they're right and that I'm
defective? Am I defective?"

Overwhelmed with pity, Sandy struggled to come up with a helpful answer. "Defective as in 'made wrong'?"

"Uh-huh." Kessa sounded a little calmer. "Made wrong. That's what I think I am."

"Made wrong sounds awfully severe and permanent to me. Maybe 'out of order' would be better."

Kessa laughed through the tears that were still trickling down her cheeks. "Yeah, that's me. I'm gonna put a sign on my door: 'out of order.' But why am I out of order? And when will I be 'back in service' again?"

"Wait a minute, Kessa. We now have three questions going at once. Let's start with the first."

The smile left her face and the tears came thicker as Kessa remembered the faces of her family during their visit.

"When Suzanna called, it made me feel like shit—excuse me. And it's even worse when all of them come into my room at once. I want to go and hide. When they leave, I hate them and I hate myself. When am I going to be able to see them and not feel that way?"

"I think that you need . . . you *all* need a referee. We call that family therapy."

There was a long silence. "You mean you want to get to know *them*? You want to talk to them like you talk to me?"

"You don't like the idea of you and me getting together to change the way you and your family act with each other?"

"What if you think that they're right? And then you might see this horrible side of me—the one that they always see. If you'd been there when I saw them today, you would hate me like they hate me." Her voice was quavery.

Sandy tried to reassure her. "If you're always going to wonder about whose side I'll take if I meet with you and your family, perhaps you should put me to the test soon."

"But first I have to know why I feel so bad about myself

when I'm with them."

"It sounds like *you* take their side when you're together."

"You wouldn't think so if you were there."

"I don't know what it looks like on the outside, but inside, you imagine what they think about you. And so that becomes what you think of yourself."

"So why do I do that?"

"Even a battered child is sure that it's his fault that his parent beats him. He hopes someday to become good enough so that the beating will stop. I guess the scariest thing for a child to believe is that a parent might be wrong about him—or her."

"So maybe they're wrong about me." Her voice perked up a little. "Does this mean I'm not defective?"

"Did they say that you are defective?"

"No, but you could see it all over their faces."

"What do you see all over their faces?"

"Well, uh . . . they look weird, and they sound weird when they talk to me."

"Maybe you're seeing frustration and confusion about you on their faces."

"Then it's still my fault?"

"What do you mean?"

"I'm a hopelessly confusing daughter."

"Confusing, but not hopelessly. You have to clarify who you are and what you're going through with your parents and your sister."

"I couldn't possibly do that," Kessa stated emphatically.

"No, but *we* could."

"How?"

"That's what family therapy is for."

Kessa came back to the present. "I get scared and angry

the minute I see my mother, before she even says anything."

"Does she do anything you can identify to provoke these feelings?"

"I'm sure she does, but not on purpose or anything. I just can't figure out what it is. And then I always . . ." She cut herself off and blushed.

"What's the matter?"

Kessa didn't reply.

Sandy tried again. "Why do you look embarrassed?"

Her face was a tell-tale giveaway whenever Kessa got embarrassed: her mouth twitched; she feigned concentration by lowering her eyebrows; she'd look anywhere—to her left, her right, at the floor—anywhere but at Sandy.

"Kessa, if you can say it, we can deal with it."

She stared at the rug and, in a hoarse whisper, said, "I still feel fat."

"Then it's still too complicated?"

"What?"

"Your life and your feelings."

"Maybe, but I *still* really feel fat. I still look at myself and hate what I see. I see a fat girl in the mirror."

"Do you feel strong when you say that to me?"

What was that supposed to mean? Was he trying to trick her? "I feel fat when I say that!"

"You sound strong when you tell me how fat you feel. It's the most confident I have ever heard you sound."

"So what?"

"So if you are the most confident about yourself when you feel fat and that makes you get the most angry and sound the toughest, it would be a great loss for you *not* to feel fat."

"I'm not lying to you. Honestly, I mean it." Her voice became weaker, as if she were trying to convince herself of the truth but was having a hard time believing it herself.

"It didn't cross my mind that you were lying. I think you

have a hard time making decisions. I think you also have a
hard time confronting people and saying what *you* think if
it's different from what *they* think. And I think that this is
the first time in your life that you've been assertive, fought
back. In a sense, this fear has become your friend."

Kessa's eyes remained focused on the floor. She felt
defeated by Sandy's statements. Whatever he said, she still
felt fat.

"And I think we have to find you better friends, kinder
friends."

"I don't want to be who I used to be before I got sick. I
don't want my old friendships back."

"What didn't you like about yourself—who you were
before you got sick?"

"I felt like I was invisible, like I was nobody. Now at least
I've got this. And maybe I've even lost it."

"You mean the anorexia?"

"When I see other girls with this on the street—really
skinny girls—I get angry at them."

"Jealous?"

"Yeah, I guess. Part of me wants to tell them that they're
stupid for doing that to themselves, and part of me still
wants to be that thin."

"It's like the difference between Francesca and Kessa,
isn't it?"

She shot him an angry glance, instantly panicking at the
sound of her old name. He'd never want her to start calling
herself Francesca again, would he? She'd been Francesca
till she got sick, and she would never call herself by that
name again, no matter how much she weighed. Francesca
was that passive, compliant kid everybody liked but nobody
really knew, the girl who couldn't challenge anyone or make
anyone unhappy. Kessa could at least be skinny, and maybe
more.

"I will always call myself Kessa," she replied icily.

"And I will always call you Kessa," he assured her.

"But I'm not sure I can be Kessa and not be thin."

"But you must be."

Surprised at his support of her name, Kessa leaned back in her chair, wanting to hear more.

"We are not meeting to fatten you up or just to maintain your weight. We meet to develop Kessa in other ways that are truly powerful. Being skinny isn't powerful—it's being frail, weak, cold, tired, too sensitive, depressed, withdrawn, and consumed with thoughts about eating and weight."

"But it's all I've got."

"Then we have to find you more."

"That's something I have to do for myself, isn't it?"

"You think of yourself as emotionally alone and unhelpable, don't you?"

"Isn't everyone?" Kessa asked sarcastically.

"Maybe we should start with what you believe people *can* do for each other."

"People can do whatever I let them do for me."

"What does that mean?"

"I think people are *there*. That's all."

"What's your connection to people?"

"Hardly any, but I don't think that they know it. There are people who've felt close to me but I never felt close to them."

"How do you make them feel close to you?"

"I can always figure out what they need. I can take good care of people."

"Without any real emotional connection on your part?"

"Yeah. No connection."

Kessa headed for Central Park, thinking that she might meet Lila again. She wasn't sure why she wanted to see her ex-roommate, but she did. She remembered Lila's laughter when she'd been playing catch with her friends. But that day had been sunny, and today was overcast and chilly and the few people walking across the park had their heads down against the wind.

Kessa made her way to the same rock where she'd been before, hoping that the girl might come by again, maybe even without her friends. She imagined a conversation in which Lila would divulge all of her secrets about how to laugh and have fun and feel safe.

Kessa sat on the rock until her toes started to get numb. Lila wasn't coming. She stood up and brushed a few dead leaves off her skirt. She would try again. Maybe tomorrow, after school.

Chapter
7

The dismissal bell rang at the fashionable and expensive Hinkley School, and the students headed for their lockers, gabbing about their homework and dates and what was happening in the city. Kessa drifted down the hallway, looking blankly at the faces passing her. The students were gathered in twos and threes. Everybody seemed to know everybody else. *Except me,* thought Kessa.

She left the building and headed west, walking slowly down three long blocks to the park. When the weather had gotten warm before her hospitalization, she'd often worn clinging halter tops. Many of the wealthy elderly women who lived on Manhattan's Upper East Side would stare at her skeletal frame. She blatantly returned their stares with a smirking grin, delighting in how openly they acknowledged their shock and revulsion at her repellent figure. *That* Kessa had loved making perfect strangers feel helpless. But now *this* Kessa's body was no longer a weapon. No one even saw her, and that only reinforced her melancholy. Kessa Dietrich was invisible and unremarkable.

Just when she thought the coast was clear—that she wouldn't see any of the "school crowd" in the neighborhood—she noticed a group of students she'd been friendly with the year before. One of them waved her over.

"Hey, Kessa, you want to go out tonight?"

There was no way to pretend she hadn't seen them. At least they all called her Kessa now. Francesca Louise was gone forever. "But it's a week night," she protested, trying to fend them off as quickly as possible.

"We're going to Skirmishes for a few hours. We won't be late."

"What's Skirmishes?"

"A bar."

"I'm sixteen."

"We're all sixteen, but they don't ask. It's fun. All the private schools go there. It's *claahsy*." The girl giggled. "So classy that they do drugs in the back. You can buy grass or coke there."

A flicker of fear passed over Kessa's features at the mention of drugs. "I think I'd better stay home. I'm behind in everything."

"You're not kidding," remarked one of the boys.

Humiliated, Kessa blushed, raised her hand in an attempt to wave goodbye, then hurried off toward the park. She crossed the meadow at Seventy-ninth Street, then went up to perch on her usual rock. From that vantage point, she saw Lila and her friends playing catch with one of the girl's shoes.

Every time the girl would get near one of the boys holding her shoes, he'd toss it to someone else and the girl would hit him in good-natured exasperation. "Oh, I give up!" she yelled, even though she was laughing, so they took pity on her and relented. She grabbed her shoe as they all sat down, still laughing.

Kessa looked at the seven of them, four boys and three girls, desperately wishing she was part of that group. Lila had not seen her.

Kessa slipped down from the rock and walked across the meadow to Central Park West. She mumbled a hello to Charles, who by now was used to her taciturnity, and rode quickly up to her floor. She threw her school books down and walked out onto the terrace overlooking the park. From her high floor she could just make out Lila and her friends. They looked like little ants scurrying around a picnic blanket.

"Kessa? Are you home?" Grace walked through the living room, feeling a draft. Honestly, it wasn't summer anymore. "Why did you leave the terrace door open? The apartment is freezing!"

"I'm sorry, Mom. I was just enjoying the view."

"All right, but please remember to close it next time." Her voice softened a little, and she tried to start a real conversation. "The buildings across the park look nice reflecting the sunset, don't they? It makes them all orange."

"Oh, I wasn't looking at them."

"What are you looking at?"

"I was watching some kids playing."

Grace looked closely at her daughter's face, feeling her usual pangs of remorse. Kessa looked so awfully wistful. Tentatively, Grace's fingers reached out to brush her daughter's hair back.

"I'm just admiring my pretty and lonesome daughter," she said softly, expecting to be rebuffed.

"I'm not so lonesome, Mommy. I have some friends. Really . . . I think you're off on the pretty part too." She shrugged.

"Well, I'm glad to hear that I'm wrong about the lonesome part, but I know I'm right about your being pretty. Though I'd be happier if you saw it too."

Kessa was tempted to yell that her mother just wanted her to be fatter, but there was so much tenderness in her mother's voice that she couldn't bring herself to do it.

"I'll help you with dinner."

Grace decided it was time to drop the fears and suspicion about being in the kitchen with her daughter. "Okay, let's roll up our sleeves." She took the veal out of the refrigerator and began breading it, leaving one piece plain for her daughter. Kessa started tearing up lettuce for the salad.

"Who were those kids you were watching in the park?" Grace asked nonchalantly.

"Just some kids who looked nice."

"Don't the kids from Hinkley look nice?"

"I guess so. I just never feel at home there."

"You used to feel at home there until—" Grace stopped herself abruptly. *Until you got anorexia.*

Kessa ignored the last statement. "I've been there since seventh grade, but it just seems like such a contest."

"A contest for what?"

Kessa frowned, not quite sure what she meant or how to explain it. "It just feels like I have to try so hard with the kids—to fit in, to be like them." She paused and took a deep breath. "Do you think I'm retarded?"

Grace brushed bread crumbs off her hands as she fought back tears. How could her daughter feel so badly about herself? First she had thought she was too fat and nearly starved herself to death. Now, after getting A's in nearly all of her classes, she was thinking she might be retarded. What other distortions did her daughter live with?

Kessa saw the look on her mother's face and added quickly: "No, Mother, I don't mean retarded like mentally retarded. I mean socially and . . . sexually. I mean, I don't really care about boys. All they do is talk about my bust anyway."

"You've got plenty of time for boys, and I'm sure you're as likable as anyone at school."

Grace didn't know what to say. She took some lemons out of the frig. Kessa's self-doubts were simply too painful for her to deal with.

"Yeah, I guess so." It was easier to back away from her mother's pain than confront what caused it. Kessa sighed as she reached for a tomato.

They continued to work in silence, each retreating behind a protective facade. Grace thought about how different her two daughters were. Suzanna—always the precocious girl—dated early and became emotionally and physically involved with boys at an age Grace had always felt was much too young. But Grace had never been able to put her foot down where Suzanna was concerned. Suzanna would look in the mirror for reassurance that she was a desirable young woman. Kessa would look in the mirror afraid that she might find traces of a woman's body. Yet even when Suzanna's behavior was at its most rebellious, Grace never felt the sense of personal rejection she got from Kessa, who wouldn't even accept the name Grace had given her. Even when her daughter was a tiny baby, no one was allowed to call her Fran or Frannie: it was always Francesca, Francesca Louise. Grace felt robbed of something intimate and loving. She thought she'd known who Francesca was. With Kessa, she never knew at all.

Chapter
8

Kessa slowly walked from school to Sandy's office, paying no attention at all to the people on the street or the inviting displays of merchandise in the store windows. She was thinking about Lila. She made up her mind that the next time she saw Lila in the park, she would approach her—no matter what. Lila would talk to her. Lila would explain how she was so confident and how Kessa could be too.

She looked up and realized she'd reached Sandy's building already. His office was one of many—there were therapists, dentists, acupuncturists, electrolysists, physicians, and even a private detective—in a large mansion that had once seen debutantes instead of patients. As she rode the maddeningly slow elevator, she thought that Sandy Sherman and Lila both knew something that she didn't. She was even toying with the idea that Sandy might share his secrets with her if she asked him.

A girl her own age walked out of Sandy's office just as she got out of the elevator. She didn't want the girl to have been Sherman's previous appointment. If she saw his other patients, she didn't feel special at all. She would often wait in the bathroom until she was a minute or two late, just so she could avoid seeing anyone else.

The waiting room was empty. Classical music was playing softly. Kessa heaved a sigh of relief and picked up a magazine. She flipped through it, looking at the food ads.

Sherman came out to the waiting room, looking calm and friendly.

"C'mon in, Kessa."

Kessa decided she was crabby. She certainly didn't have to hide it from him.

"What's the matter?" He picked up on her mood immediately.

"I just feel that I can't be *me* most of the time."

"Are you *you* right now?"

"Yes. Creepy, isn't it?"

"Not for me. I don't experience you as creepy. Just in a bad mood."

"Don't you think it's terrible that I am sitting in your office ruining your day?"

"You're not ruining my day. Your bad mood is not *my* bad mood."

Kessa looked at him suspiciously. What was *that* supposed to mean? "You don't care if I'm in a bad mood?"

"I'd like you to feel better, but bad moods are a part of life. They're not the end of the world."

"How come if I cry at home, my mother cries too? Even when she doesn't, she looks like she's about to."

"How do you feel when she cries?"

"I don't see her cry so much. But if I think she might cry, I try to stop her."

"Why?"

"Because it's mean to let her feel bad."

Sherman didn't quite understand her logic. "Are you saying that it's mean to *make* her feel bad?"

"What's the difference?"

"If you make her feel bad, then you've done something to her—you've hurt her. If she feels bad for a reason that has nothing to do with you, then her bad mood is not your responsibility."

"But I always feel like her moods are my responsibility. When they're bad, I get scared and feel I have to cheer her up."

"Is that why you think your mood might ruin *my* day?"

She nodded her head, embarrassed. She might as well just come out and say Sandy might be as important to her as her mother.

"We all see the important people in our lives in a perspective similar to the way we view our parents. If you're afraid you'll ruin your mother's day, it makes sense that you'd be afraid you'll ruin mine too. You and I have an important relationship, and it has to be powerful enough to help you make changes in your life."

Kessa thought about that for a minute. "Okay. I don't feel like my bad mood could ruin your day anymore. Is that bad?"

"No. It means that you're beginning to be able to tell where you end and I begin."

"So I could be upset and it wouldn't mess you up?"

Sherman smiled and nodded.

"Why does that make me feel good?" Kessa asked.

"Because you've just discovered that you don't have to take responsibility for me."

"Does that mean I'm lazy?"

"I think you've got behaving responsibly mixed up with being responsible for people."

"I always think I'm responsible for everybody around
me."

"That must make you mad."

"Why?"

"Being responsible for people is a job as well as a relationship. And if you're 'on' all the time, it could make you
overworked. You might get a little angry at the people who
are overworking you."

"I'm doing it to myself, though."

"Then maybe we'll have to find out why, so we can get
you off your own back."

When the change-of-class bell rang, Kessa gathered her
books and headed for the locker room to get ready for gym.
She used to look forward to changing in the locker room
when other girls stole shocked glances at her emaciated
body last spring. Now they would look at her and think she
was fat—just as fat as all the other girls, maybe even fatter.
Nothing separated her from the parade of thunder thighs
trooping up the stairs from the locker room to the gym.

"Hi, Kessa. You look good!"

"Hi, Kessa. You look like you put on some weight."

"Hey, Francesca. Filling out, huh?"

Her classmates meant well, but the comments stung her
as if they were all mockery. *Filling out*. That meant she was
turning into a tub of lard. Kessa decided to join the gymnastics squad so that all the hideous pounds of flab on her body
would at least turn into muscle.

Kessa reached the gym. Actually, the gym was a former
ballroom with arched eight-foot French windows opposite a
wall of mirrors, where a ballet bar had been added. It was
up on the third floor of the renovated townhouse that was
now the Hinkley School.

Kessa was surrounded by mirrors and other girls. She saw

her body reflected down the length of the room and her heart started pounding. She'd just leave, run out. But then she remembered how many calories exercise could burn up . . .

The instructor clapped her hands and announced, "All right, girls. Now we'll do a series of warm-ups to firm up and then a series of stretches to loosen up. *Remember*—our bodies are the tools we use to achieve gymnastic excellence!"

Kessa looked down at her own body. She wished she'd never gained back the weight. She wanted her old "tool" back, the thin one. *The thinner is the winner.*

Chapter 9

As Kessa lay in her bed that night, she remembered the bed in the hospital. She remembered how it had always hurt a bit no matter which way she positioned herself. She would anticipate the pain. If she lay on her back, her shoulder blades, lower back, and the bottom of her spine would hurt. Sometimes she would spend extra time in the bath just to feel the pressure of her spine against the porcelain tub. If she lay on her side, her hip and shoulder hurt. She began to be reassured by these pains, tangible symbols of her success in becoming thinner than anyone else. Her only identity was being "the skinniest." She had to *feel* it. Some days she even adjusted the hospital bed to aggravate the pain. That made her feel even thinner. *The thinner is the winner.* After she was put on intravenous feeding—gaining weight no matter what—she nearly put her back out of alignment one day by raising the center of the bed and putting her left hip on top of the miniature hill she had created.

She remembered the very first doctor who'd come to examine her in the hospital, even before Dr. Jarvis, her chief resident, had come in. He'd sauntered in and said, "I'll be following you for this month."

"This month? How long will I be here?"

"That's up to your attending."

"What's an attending?"

"Oh." Of course he assumed that everyone understood medical jargon. "You see, at a teaching hospital, one affiliated with a medical school, there is your regular doctor, a resident, who's in charge of the service—pediatrics, in this case—and an intern, who follows the patient for a month. We get shipped to a different part of the hospital each month for a year, and all of us are supervised by the chairman or chief of the service."

He was boyishly handsome, and Kessa could tell he wanted to impress her. But he probably tried to impress everybody. He didn't even know who she was.

"Which one are you?"

"I'm the intern, Dr. Laslow, but everybody in pediatrics calls me Dr. Max. That's my first name."

Kessa faked a smile and tried to relax.

"Now I have to ask you a bunch of questions, which we ask every new patient here unless he or she is too young to talk yet."

Kessa wanted to laugh, but she was worried about his questions.

They looked at each other warily for what seemed like ages. Kessa couldn't bear it. "Well, I guess you should start and get it over with."

"First, why are you being hospitalized?"

She looked down at the sheets. She didn't want to tell him, but she was afraid not to. "I have anorexia nervosa."

"How long have you had it?"

She shot him a defiant glance. "Look, I'm not even sure that I have it."

Her response took him aback. "Well, let's see. Have you lost twenty-five percent of your body weight?"

"Probably."

"Have you stopped menstruating?"

That wasn't any of his business. She picked at the sheets some more. "Yes," she muttered.

"Are you constipated?"

This was too humiliating to even answer. She nodded.

"Have you grown any additional body hair?"

She was so surprised that he should know about that, that she nodded again.

"Have you become more withdrawn and depressed lately?"

"Um-hmm."

"Are you still trying to lose more weight or maintain your present weight?"

"Well, I'm not looking to get fat."

"From your answers, you seem to have A.N. all right."

She didn't like him at all. How could he just barge in here, invade her privacy, and then mechanically size her up like she was some textbook or something?

"Could you leave me alone now?"

"I still need more personal history."

"Oh, all right." She refused to meet his eyes.

He asked about her living arrangement, if anyone else in the family had ever had psychological problems, where she went to school, how she got along with her friends, what she thought about her appearance. Idiotic questions. Why didn't he just call up her mother and ask her?

"Are you finished?" she finally asked in exasperation.

"Yes. You've been very cooperative. Thanks. See you later. 'Bye." He cheerily walked out the door.

Kessa opened her mouth in shock. He'd been completely indifferent to her sulking. She leaned back on her hospital bed, overwhelmed with depression. She'd been abandoned, left helpless among strangers who just didn't care.

That had been months ago. Now she remembered her therapist saying the sentence—those five words—that began to turn her against the comfort of the illness: "You live a small life."

It all came back to her.

She'd looked at him, unable to challenge his logic, and started to cry.

He handed her a tissue. "We'll have to find you a larger life, Kessa."

She was suddenly mad at her bones. Maybe he was right. Maybe all they were worth was a small life.

"Maybe I'm scared of a bigger life."

"Scared doesn't mean you can't have it."

"How can I do what I'm scared of doing?"

Sandy could barely hear her. Her voice had become as small and weak as her body. "I'll help you be scared."

"I don't want help. And I don't think you help a person by making her scared."

"You're more than scared. You're frightened of feeling scared. I guess it's frightening for you to *feel*. It's safer for you to be numb, separate, and lonely."

Kessa's face went blank.

"You see what you've just done to feel safe from me?" Sandy asked.

There was nothing to say. Kessa stared straight ahead.

Sandy made a ridiculous face at her, and when she didn't even blink, he touched the tip of her nose and pushed it a bit. "This may be the softest part of you." He smiled, still teasing.

"Leave me alone. I want to be mad at you."

"No. I won't leave you alone, and I won't let you get mad at me."

"How can you stop me?"

"I already have."

"What did you mean before about helping me be scared? It didn't sound like such a good idea, you know."

"If you don't trust anyone, that includes yourself. I can get scared, knowing that unless my life and safety are in danger, it's only a matter of time and what I do until the fear subsides. If I can't help myself, I can at least turn to others for help."

"So I don't trust anyone else, but I trust myself."

"If you trusted yourself, Kessa, you could be flexible. You wouldn't believe that if you didn't stay a skeleton, you'd automatically be a blimp. You don't trust yourself to do anything but to be thin."

"And you're taking that away!" Kessa stared at the blanket, afraid of him because his simple, quiet logic made sense. But if *Sandy* made sense, then her illness *didn't* make sense. She placed one of her hands on her pelvic blade, seeking the reassurance that it still protruded.

Sandy noticed the gesture. "If only the bone could talk back to you and tell you it would take care of you and keep you safe."

"It's all I've got."

"Then let's find you more."

"How do I know that if I give this up I'll have more?"

"If you don't give it up, Kessa, you can't ever have more."

"So there's no guarantee?"

"You will discover your own strengths and resources if you are deprived of your skinniness for security."

"You want me to give up my only security?"

"So that you can have more from other sources."

"Why can't I get these other sources of security *first*?" she protested.

"Can you talk a junkie out of heroin while he's stoned? Can you talk the public into driving smaller cars if they have all the cheap gas they want?"

"You mean I'm going to have to go cold turkey? And feel deprived all the time?"

"If we don't have to change self-destructive or wasteful patterns, we won't. But basically we are resourceful creatures, and if we can tolerate deprivation and fear, we can also change and learn how to have more healthy behavior and different values."

"That's easy for *you* to say. You don't have to change anything."

"Everything that happens between us is easier for me than for you. I'm always aware of that. It doesn't mean that we can excuse you from the necessary struggling you have to do. But I don't want you to think that your struggles and fears won't be noticed, or not appreciated or not supported."

"So you're going to help me struggle and be scared. Big deal. I think that's the worst offer anybody ever made me!" But she managed a smile.

Kessa stared at the ceiling. Her bed at home was more comfortable than the bed in the hospital had ever been. She felt for her pelvic blade, for reassurance that she was still thin. Only the tip of it still protruded. "The rest of it is covered with fat," she mumbled aloud. "He stole my skinniness away. Lila doesn't like me and I'll never see her again and I still don't belong anywhere. I hate my body. A woman's body . . . looks so stupid."

Chapter
10

The dismissal bell rang. As usual, most of the students raced to their lockers, chattering about their classes or who was going out with whom and where everyone was going to be hanging out.

And as usual, Kessa slowly gathered her books, lingering behind her classmates, hoping for a conversation she could join. She told herself that she'd just have to get used to becoming more social, just as she'd just had to get used to the plastic tubing that had been implanted in her chest for seven weeks. Kessa almost laughed at her chain of thought—from induced feedings in the hospital to the Hinkley School. But maybe that connection wasn't so strange after all. Being forced to gain weight had been the greatest fear she'd had, and she guessed becoming part of the social scene was next.

As Kessa walked to her locker, she was surprised by the smiles flashed at her by three girls huddled in the hallway.

"Hey, Kessa," one of them called to her. "Last week we

went to Skirmishes and it was pretty okay. You wanna come with us tonight?"

Kessa's heart began to race. *Try,* she told herself, *you have to try.* She nodded vigorously so she wouldn't have to say anything. She'd never keep the tremor out of her voice.

"Great. Meet you on Seventy-second and Lex at eight o'clock."

Kessa had eaten her carefully measured dinner slowly: sliced turkey, a scoop of brown rice, and a large salad— spartan but adequate. Lots of fiber that didn't have very many calories.

"Mom, I'd like to go out with some friends tonight," she blurted suddenly.

Grace was surprised. It was the first time her daughter mentioned getting together with school friends since she'd left the hospital. "Why, I'm sure that would be very nice," she said, swallowing her doubts. "Just don't be out too late."

The entrance to Skirmishes was flanked by two antique lanterns. They made Kessa nervous. The brass looked so old, so distinguished, that Kessa felt even younger in comparison. What if someone asked for identification and made her leave?

Kessa's three companions acted like they lived in the place, walking nonchalantly through the narrow entrance hall that was paneled with dark wood. Since they'd been there before, it was easy to show off in front of the uninitiated.

Just try, Kessa kept repeating over and over to herself. Then she remembered one of her conversations with Sherman: "I guess I'll just have to do this scared," she mumbled.

"Did you ask for something?" Susan turned to her.

Kessa hadn't realized she'd spoken aloud. Luckily, they

couldn't see her blush in the dim light of the bar. "No, I was just wondering about the service."

Susan giggled. "Kessa, we don't come here for the service. That's for a restaurant . . . not a dump like this. We come here to cool out."

Kessa blushed again. She wanted to ask why they wanted to cool out in a bar when one of the girls poked her and said, "Isn't he fabulous? I'd like to get a hold of him later!"

Kessa finally realized why they were cooling out. To meet guys or—even worse—men!

"There's a table for four and it's near the bar. Quick!"

Susan locked elbows with Kessa and dragged her to a table where they could check out everyone who walked in— and be checked out as well. Kessa took it all in, feeling like she was in a zoo. On the wrong side of the cage.

When Kessa told Sandy about Skirmishes the next afternoon in his office, her fists clenched until the knuckles were white.

"When two guys came up to the table, I just wanted to leave. I mean, I was too scared to leave and too scared to stay. So I got up and went to the ladies' room. I'm only sixteen, and everybody else my age is interested in guys. So that means I can't be friends with anyone. If it's a girl, then we have to go looking for guys, and if it's a guy, he doesn't just want to be friends. What's the matter with everybody?"

Sherman sat quietly, watching her. Kessa's face was so open sometimes. It was as if she'd hit an instant replay button in her head and heard the entire outburst all over again.

"Are you feeling like everyone is out of step with you?" Sandy ventured.

"Look, I know it's me." She stared at the floor. To Sandy, she just seemed to blank out.

"Kessa, where have you gone? What are you thinking about?"

"I'm thinking about how I don't want to talk about this."

"If you don't, no one will make you."

"Why did I have to be a girl?"

"Do you want to be a boy?"

"Maybe."

"Why?"

"It seems like a better deal." She thought for a minute about her brother, Gregg—the great student, athlete, son, the golden boy who did no wrong, the golden boy who never bothered to visit her in the hospital or call her when she'd been released. She'd written him a long letter venting her frustrated rage and he'd never even bothered to reply, so she'd just written him off altogether.

"Are there things you like about being a boy, or are there things you dislike about being a girl?"

"I'm going to get my period back soon, right?"

"Probably. I guess you're telling me you don't want it."

"The whole idea bugs me."

"Does the physical part of it bother you . . . the bleeding? Even though I'm a man, I'm not foolish enough to think that it's fun."

"Well it is a pain, but that's not why I don't want it."

"Do you know why you don't want it?"

"It reminds me that I'm supposed to be grown up, an adult, a—"

"A woman?"

"A woman," she echoed, making a face. "It seems like such a stupid idea. If my period comes back, I'm going to want to lose weight again to make it go away."

"Is that why you lost your weight to begin with?"

"No. I didn't even know that would happen till Dr. Gordon mentioned it, but after it did, I liked it."

"If a girl gets her period at ten, she's not a woman. She's a ten-year-old girl with a period," he countered.

"But it's like an announcement. It reminds you that you're gonna be a woman whether you want to or not."

"Then it reminds you to fear the future?"

"Pretty much."

"Who might you become in the future?"

"What do you mean?"

"Who is the unhappy woman you don't want to become?"

"You mean like somebody I know now?"

He nodded.

"I don't want to become middle-aged and fat and ... depressed."

"Who do you know that's middle-aged and depressed?"

She hesitated. "I think my mother is. I don't want to become her. I think that she's nice and she's kind, but I don't want her life."

"You don't have to inherit her life."

"Yes I do."

"You've never described your mother as depressed before."

"I don't know if that's the right word or not. There's just something missing in her life. I don't know what it is, but I wish she had it. I wish I could give it to her."

"Does your father have what you'd like to give to your mother?"

"I don't know if he's happy. He drinks a lot when he's home. He works really hard. He's got this big business he built up by himself, and people work for him and his name is on doors and stationery and people respect him, and I'd rather be him than her."

"Is it the same for the other women in your family?"

"Fat chance! Suzanna walked out on the whole deal. She got away from my father, and nobody tells her what to do.

Nobody *ever* told her what to do." Kessa looked out at the darkening sky. "It's as if my mother never got away."

"From what?"

"Not from what. From who!"

Sandy waited for her to explain.

"From my grandmother—her mother. She still runs there all the time. It's like *my* mother's still waiting for *her* mother to let her . . . oh, I don't know. I just know that she's always running to her mother's house and my mother is in her fifties. When I'm in *my* fifties I don't want to be running to *my* mother's house every time I have an hour to spare. I guess that's why Suzanna moved to California."

"I guess you're hoping that if you don't get your period you can feel like your own person."

Kessa didn't like Sherman's interpretation. She was doing things that made her feel safe, but he was trying to expose them as unnatural, sick even. She didn't answer him.

"You didn't like what I said."

Silence.

"I don't think I'd like to hear that either," Sandy said.

Leave me alone! Kessa thought fiercely. *Let me sulk in peace. I earned the right to mope this time.* She wanted Sandy to apologize for daring to explain her private pain to her. At that moment, she wanted never to have to agree with him again.

"I think this session has been pretty rough. We could end five minutes early if you like."

She was dying to leave—to walk out on him. She also wanted to sit for five more minutes in absolute silence, not deigning to look in his direction, wanting him to look at least a little guilty. She glanced at the clock, waited two minutes, then walked out and slammed the door.

There was a brisk, cool breeze and the skies were threatening as Kessa waited for the crosstown bus. Funny how she had mentioned her brother. She almost never thought of him anymore. *He sure never thinks about me,* she told herself ruefully. *Never has and never will.* Gregg thought about Gregg, and Mom and Dad always encouraged that. So now what do they get for all their affection?

The bus lumbered into view, and Kessa absently took a seat. *My own brother,* she thought, *is a real shithead.* She almost smiled at the word. *He isn't really even my brother anymore. I wonder what it would be like to have a real brother, someone who'd talk to me about girls, about growing up, about having fun . . .*

Someone was saying something.

"Excuse me." The person sitting next to her was talking. "Sorry, but this is my stop."

Kessa blushed and mumbled an apology as she stood up. As the stranger passed her, their eyes met. It was a guy who looked like he was about Gregg's age, maybe younger. And he blushed.

Kessa sat down by the window and felt a shiver of amazement. A guy had blushed because of her! Maybe he thought he'd stepped on her toe or something.

She nearly smiled again. Where was Gregg when she needed him? Who was going to teach her how to live?

Chapter
11

Kessa was glad to see that several new students had joined
her gymnastics class. It was nervewracking to feel like the
newest and most inexperienced member.

The students lined up in a semicircle around the instructor at the high bar. One of the new students stood out. Not
only was she tall, but she was thin. Suspiciously thin. The
outline of her chest bones showed under her thin cotton t-
shirt, and her arms were like sticks. Kessa felt a hot surge of
rage. It wasn't fair. She had given in, surrendering to the
demand that she gain weight, while this other girl was a
holdout, lasting longer than Kessa . . . defeating her. *The
thinner is the winner.*

Kessa watched closely when it was the new girl's turn to
mount. She hardly had the strength to climb onto the high
bar. The instructor looked at her closely and suggested that
the girl strengthen her arm muscles by doing twenty push-
ups a day for at least a week or two. The new girl nodded
blankly.

During the free exercise period, Kessa's eyes never left

the new girl. As if aware that she was being watched, she
went to a corner of the room and positioned herself diago-
nally with her head pointed to the corner. She took a deep
breath and tried to do a push-up. After the third uneven
attempt, she dropped to the mat, unable to do any more.
Kessa watched, biting her lip, feeling sorry for the new girl
but secretly glad that she was such a weakling. She must be
a "skinny," as Lila would have said, a poor, crazy skinny.

Kessa had to know for sure.

She sauntered over to the new girl, who was sitting up on
the mat, breathing rapidly. Her face was flushed a deep
crimson from exertion.

"Hi! My names's Kessa. Welcome to the class." Kessa
was surprised by her own outgoingness.

The girl looked exhausted and embarrassed and shy. "I'm
not very good at this. Oh, my name's Deirdre."

"That's funny. My last name's Dietrich. Sounds almost
like your first name."

"I hope your name is luckier than mine. Deirdre means
'daughter of sorrows.' "

Kessa's eyes widened. That was a pretty weird thing to
admit to someone you'd just met. Deirdre must have some
heavy-duty problems, and Kessa had the instinctive feeling
she knew what a lot of them were.

"Oh, we're all daughters of some sorrow or other," she
said, thinking of her last meeting with Sherman.

"What sorrow are you the daughter of?"

Kessa was not quite ready to talk about herself with some
new girl. She ignored the question.

"Hey, let me show you how to hold your hands so you can
do push-ups without your wrists twisting."

"My wrists don't twist," Deirdre protested.

"Well, when you're doing push-ups, you have three sets of

muscles you can pull from: chest, shoulders, and triceps. If you spread out the strain, you'll last longer."

Deirdre tried again, following Kessa's directions. She barely made two push-ups. On the third, her face turned nearly purple and her arms caved in. She fell face forward on the mat and lay there panting for a few seconds. Then she looked up apologetically.

"Well, that does feel better. Thanks, Kessa."

It was nice to have someone like her right away. "Hey, Deirdre What's-your-name, why don't you come to my house after school?"

"It's Deirdre McGuire, and I'd love to."

As the two girls walked out of the elevator, Kessa realized she'd left her key in another bag. "Shoot," she said. "Let's hope my mother is home, or we're locked out and I'll owe you an invitation."

"Oh, that'll be all right. I do that all the time," Deirdre said quickly in a tone that was so anxiously reassuring Kessa was instantly exasperated. She leaned on the doorbell.

Grace opened the door, surprised to see her daughter with a friend.

"Hi, Mom. This is Deirdre McGuire."

Deirdre took a deep breath, reached for Grace's hand, and shook it vigorously. She flashed a broad grin and introduced herself in a voice that seemed much too large for her body.

"Hello, Mrs. Dietrich. I'm glad to meet you."

As the pair walked off toward Kessa's room, Grace's initial pleasure at Kessa's friendship with this outgoing girl faded when she noticed Deirdre's body. She was as thin as a toothpick.

Grace walked into her own bedroom and sat down in an

overstuffed chair, her heart racing. She picked up a magazine, leafed through a few pages, then threw it down in
frustration. She was too keyed up to read anything. Anxious
thoughts repeated themselves over and over in her head as if
looped audiotape were stuck on PLAY.

Can a thinner girl with anorexia cause a nearly recovered
girl to slide back into it? she wondered. Does Kessa want to
help this girl or imitate her? Is Deirdre just a normal girl
who's a bit on the thin side and am I exaggerating? When
will we *all* be over this?

Grace couldn't stand it any longer. She hurried over to
her daughter's door and knocked.

"Come in," Kessa said in a perfectly normal voice.

The two girls were sitting on the floor, plowing through a
pile of records. Harmless enough, Grace thought, heaving a
sigh of relief. Maybe she was just imagining things.

"What is it, Mom?"

"I was wondering if you two would like a snack."

The tense silence that followed confirmed all her fears.
No one knew what to say. After what seemed like endless
seconds, Kessa replied for both of them.

"Thanks, maybe later."

Grace got the hint. As she closed the door, she replied
over her shoulder, "Just let me know."

The girls stared at each other, both waiting for the other
to speak.

"Are you on a diet?" Kessa blurted.

"Sort of."

"What's your goal weight?"

Deirdre was startled, so she answered truthfully. "A few
pounds less than this."

"How much do you weigh?"

"Hey, you're beginning to sound like my mother!"

"You mean your mother is trying to stop you from losing

weight?"

"Yeah, sometimes, but why all the questions?"

Kessa took a long look at Deirdre before making a decision. "Because I just got out of the hospital."

"Oh, what for?"

"Losing too much weight."

What seemed like a disclosure to Kessa felt like an accusation to Deirdre. "I don't want to lose too much weight," she protested.

"Neither did I."

Deirdre started to fidget. "I guess I ought to be going home now."

"Listen, I'm not mad at you or anything. I think you're on your way to a dangerous place I just got back from." Kessa was surprised that her own anger sounded familiar. Just, in fact, like her mother's. "I know how it seems like you want to lose only a few more pounds, until you're nearly dead and you still want to lose a few more. If they hadn't hooked me up to a machine that force-fed me intravenously, I'd probably be dead by now. And don't think it's so easy for me to say that. It isn't. I haven't told this to anybody else."

Deirdre grabbed her books and purse and stood up. "I've really got to go now." Tears were filling her eyes.

Kessa bit her lip, remembering the shame she'd felt when anyone tried to confront her about her own weight loss.

"Okay. I'll see you tomorrow in gym, all right?"

"Sure. See ya." She hurried out.

Kessa heard the false cheeriness in Deirdre's voice as she said goodbye to Grace.

"Why, goodbye . . . Deirdre. It's been nice meeting you," answered a perplexed Grace. She'd almost forgotten this girl's name. Grace walked over to Kessa's room, where her daughter sat absently shelving her records.

"Deirdre seems pleasant."

"She's nice, Mom. But something about her bothers me."

"What?"

"She's got strange habits. You know the little end table near my bed? Well, while we were talking, she took a tissue and polished the tops of the chrome legs. She tried to make a joke out of it, but I think that she *had* to do that. It was like she was obsessed or something. She also arranged things on my desk. I didn't really mind, but I thought that she'd end up dusting the blinds if she stayed long enough. She didn't mess up my things or anything but she just couldn't help it. It upset me, but I'm not sure why."

Grace was so relieved when Kessa confessed her reaction that her heart stopped thumping. "Maybe that's what she does before she gets comfortable with a new friend. Sort of a nervous habit."

"Mmm." Kessa didn't believe it for a second. She thought of her counting games—how she'd divide everything, her self-imposed rules and regulations—and changed the subject. "When will dinner be ready?"

"As soon as your father gets home."

"She makes me so angry." Kessa was sitting opposite Sherman, his coffee table between them as usual.

"Why?"

"Because she's just like I was and she's pretending she's not."

"Any other reason you're angry at her?"

"What do you mean?"

"Does it bother you that she's still the way you used to be?"

"You mean am I jealous?" Kessa made a face. "I don't want to be like that anymore," she protested a little too loudly. "But I don't want anybody else to be like that either, I guess."

"Why don't you want anybody else to be like that either?"

"It's horrible to be like that!"

Sandy looked skeptical.

"All right," Kessa said after making another face at him. "I don't want anybody to have what I had to give up. Are you happy now?"

"What did you give up?"

"You know, being special."

"Then it still feels like a loss?"

"Sometimes." She stared at the floor, her usual depressed posture. "You know," she mumbled, still not meeting his eyes, "sometimes I'm really sorry I'm not skinny anymore. Sometimes I think I'm fat and ugly. You said I would feel better once I gained my weight back. How come I still have these bad feelings now that I look normal?"

"You're mad because I convinced you to gain weight?"

"I'm mad because you made me give up something I wanted to keep. Sometimes it feels like you stole it from me."

"Why did we agree that it would be better for you if you were able to regain your weight?"

Kessa heaved an exaggeratedly loud sigh. "You said that there was no way of feeling better if I didn't, and there was no guarantee, but no chance at all if I didn't."

"So you feel that I betrayed you?"

Kessa looked up from the floor. "No, I just hate it when I see Deirdre and feel sorry for her, but I'm still jealous of her at the same time. It's like I *want* her to do badly so I don't feel I made a mistake in gaining weight."

"Do you miss being so thin?"

"Once in a while. The other day I was looking in the mirror. It was after Deirdre left. I looked so bland—so nothing. Like anybody else. None of my chest bones showed.

I used to love to feel all my bones. I pointed one shoulder toward the mirror. I remembered when you said I was still too skinny because my shoulder bones stuck out so much. When I looked in the mirror, I could still see a little bit of the notch the bones make there." She caressed the bone. "I was relieved and felt stupid at the same time. When is this all gonna go away?"

"Has it diminished any in the last six months?"

"Yeah, I suppose, but it still comes and goes. I just wish it wouldn't ever come back again."

"I think we all change and heal and grow in the uneven way you're describing."

"So what can I do for Deirdre? Most of the time I hate to see her stuck in this craziness."

"I guess you'll just have to try to be friends without forgetting where you end and she begins."

"I'll try," Kessa said. She felt her collarbone again. "It's still a little bumpy, you know."

"Maybe it's chicken pox."

Chapter
12

Once a month Kessa walked east on Seventy-second Street for her check-up with Dr. Gordon, her physician. Those visits used to be once a week when the threat of hospitalization had been hanging over her head like a guillotine about to fall.

Kessa found herself whistling as she walked, but as soon as she saw Deirdre sitting on one of the armchairs, the tune faded from her lips. She turned to leave, then resolutely forced herself to walk directly up to Deirdre.

"Hi. Are you here for a school check-up?"

Deirdre paled in shock. What was Kessa doing here? Her mind raced to find a casual answer. *No, I'm not here for a school check-up, but I'm not about to admit why I am here.* "Actually, I've been feeling run-down. You remember, in the gym, I could hardly even do a push-up."

"Yeah, maybe you need some vitamins." Kessa sat down next to Deirdre and took out a book. End of confrontation.

Dr. Gordon's receptionist walked into the waiting room, a manila file in her hand.

"Deirdre McGuire," she announced.

Deirdre got up slowly, waved to Kessa, and walked toward the hall leading to the examining rooms. Kessa stared after her, wondering how long she had been Dr. Gordon's patient and if she too would be forced to go to the hospital. They'd probably cut her chest open and stick in a tube that would pour calories into her. Then maybe she'd get better. Maybe she wouldn't. There were times, Kessa remembered, when she just couldn't handle anything, and the infusion pump was her worst enemy. It made her lose her wonderful bones. It made her fat.

"Hello." A wooden, formal voice answered.

"Dr. Sherman?" Maybe she'd misdialed.

"Kessa?"

"Yes. I just wanted to ask you something."

"I'm in session right now, but I can call you back in half an hour. Okay?"

"Oh. Sure."

She hung up, feeling rejected and frustrated as usual.

A few minutes later, she angrily buzzed for the nurse. Laura, the "primary nurse," came in. During the day shift she'd have most of the responsibility of coping with Kessa.

"Good morning, Kessa. By the way, I notice that your chart says Francesca Louise Dietrich. That's a fancy name. How come you changed it to Kessa?"

"I never liked that name—especially the way my mother says it."

"Suit yourself. I like both."

"Do you know how much weight I'm going to gain this week?"

"How many calories a day are you getting?"

"Two thousand!" Kessa shouted.

Laura was not impressed with the amount Kessa regarded

as gargantuan. "How many calories are you eating per day?"

"None. I'd be crazy to eat on top of all these calories."

"Kessa, with a normal metabolism, you need one thousand calories a day just to maintain seventy pounds. Each five hundred calories puts one pound a week on you. So, to answer your question, two thousand calories a day puts two pounds a week on you plus whatever it takes to make up for any dehydration you started with."

"What do you mean about dehydration?" Was that some sort of trick?

"When you came in here you were dry—you didn't have the proper amount of water in your system. In the first week your system could absorb as much as eight pounds of water from the IV fluids."

"That means I could gain as much as ten pounds in a week!"

"It means you could gain eight pounds of fluid, but only two real pounds."

"I don't care what you call it! I don't want to gain ten pounds this week!"

There had been some anorectic patients on the floor before, but at some point Laura invariably found it hard to supply the infinite patience they seemed to require. She stared at this ranting skeleton of a girl, fighting so hard to prevent weight from being added to a body that had nearly wasted away to nothing. It was so incredibly frustrating.

"Kessa, do you know what you look like?"

"I know that I'm getting fat at the speed of light!"

Laura took the bait. "Where do you think you're getting fat?"

"I can *feel* it . . . all over. My legs, my stomach, my arms."

Laura shook her head. "That's impossible. You're gaining

it *nowhere,* Kessa. I'm afraid you're still the skeleton you were when you came here a week ago."

"Well, I want this thing taken out or changed so that I don't gain weight faster than I can handle it."

"I'm afraid you'll have to talk that over with Dr. Donaldson, your internist. I don't make those kinds of decisions around here. I'll call him and he'll be in touch with you. See you later."

Kessa felt like she'd just been hung up on. Again. First Sherman couldn't talk to her, then the nurse had to leave after telling her she could gain ten pounds in a week.

"Nobody cares about me!" she shouted at the ceiling. Luckily, Lila was in physical therapy all afternoon.

The phone rang. She picked it up, ready to yell at whoever it was.

"Hello, Kessa?"

"Well, it's about time you called me back!" Kessa was surprised by the shrill anger in her voice.

"Why are you angry? I said that I'd call you back as soon as I could, and I have."

Kessa was immediately contrite. "I—um, I'm gaining weight faster than I'm comfortable with, and I don't think that it's a good idea."

Sherman had to pause for a minute, needing to resolve this problem. It was a matter of ethics. She was an adolescent psychiatric patient on a medical floor, and she wanted her medical treatment altered for emotional reasons.

"Kessa, the fluid flow you're now receiving will only put on two pounds a week. There'll be some daily variation, depending upon how much water you retain."

Sandy's calm tone rekindled her anger. "I don't know what all that means. All I do know is that I'm getting too fat too fast! I gained a whole pound just between yesterday and today."

Sandy waited for her to calm down a bit. "How much weight have you gained in the past seven days?"

"I gained one whole pound in twenty-four hours!"

"How much have you gained in the past seven days?" he repeated.

"Two pounds. But I'm gaining faster now."

"Kessa, I know this is a hard thing for you to go through. But if we wait for you to gain what you say is 'comfortable,' we may be waiting forever. Having to gain any weight will always be hard and scary, so you might as well start getting used to it now. No one who's been addicted to a substance, a behavior, or an idea ever gave it up comfortably. Now is as good a time—"

He heard the click as she hung up on him.

"Francesca Dietrich."

Someone was calling her name.

"Miss Dietrich."

Kessa came down to earth. Nearly fifteen minutes had passed and Dr. Gordon's receptionist was calling her.

"Sorry, I was daydreaming," Kessa said as she hurried off to one of the examining rooms.

She hated being called Francesca. This would have to be straightened out immediately.

"Well, dear, you continue to look fine," Dr. Gordon greeted her.

The doctor's bedside manner was a constant calm, whether dealing with an emergency or Kessa's gradual recovery. She was always the same warmly matter-of-fact army sergeant who'd shipped a sixty-nine pound Kessa off to the hospital the previous spring.

"Yes, you look very good."

Fat, Kessa instinctively thought to herself.

"Are you feeling as good as you look?"

"Sometimes. I'm glad *you're* happy with the way I look."

That bit of sarcasm was not what the doctor wanted to hear. "Frankly, Francesca, you could stand to gain a few more pounds."

"Dr. Gordon, my friends all call me Kessa now."

"I'll take that as a flattering invitation, Kessa."

"Has Deirdre McGuire been your patient long?"

"Confidential information, Kessa."

"I just met her last week. She goes to my school. I think she's anorectic."

"Let's hope she isn't." Dr. Gordon couldn't keep the concern out of her voice.

"Is there anything I can do?"

"Kessa, that's very considerate of you, but when it comes to anorexia, I'm not even sure there's much I can do. If you recall, when you were losing weight I didn't sense much ability on my part to stop it."

"I guess kids can be stubborn, huh?"

"I never regarded you as stubborn, my dear. I think it's far more complex than that—for you or anyone else who has this problem." She smiled.

Kessa smiled back. Dr. Gordon was no longer the enemy. She was an ally, and Kessa was glad. She'd missed that relationship for nearly a year.

Chapter
13

Deirdre was the first to arrive in the locker room. She went right to the toilet and threw up her lunch with virtually effortless efficiency that came only after months of experience. Her stomach would be flat—and empty—for gymnastic class.

Kessa was the second to arrive, in time to hear the toilet flushing and see pale and puffy-eyed Deirdre hurrying out of the girls' room.

Seeing Kessa rattled Deirdre's nerves. That girl had a knack for showing up everywhere. It was like she was a spy or something.

"Boy, you're early," Deirdre said, sounding annoyed.

"Not as early as you."

"Are you mad at me for something?"

"Deirdre, are you losing weight?"

Now Kessa sounded just like Deirdre's own mother. Same dumb accusing question. She started to shout, but anger would be a dead giveaway, right? Instead, she fought to keep her voice even. "Why is it any of your bus— Would you be mad at me for losing weight?"

"No. I guess I couldn't be mad at you for that, but I could sure get frustrated with you if I thought you were stuck losing weight."

"What do you mean—'stuck'?"

"I can't believe you don't know what I mean."

"Everybody tries to lose weight. What's the big deal?"

"Some people try too hard, and they use weird ways to do it. They take laxatives and make themselves throw up and just plain starve."

Kessa noticed Deirdre's eyes widen in fright when she mentioned throwing up. So that was why Deirdre always left the lunchroom early, why Deirdre always got to the locker room first.

"I just hope you're not on an anorectic trip. It's pretty horrible. I've been there and it just gets worse." This admission made Kessa feel funny, as usual, but she desperately wanted to confront Deirdre. She wanted to shake her and scream at her and try and make her understand. Kessa was the only one who could truly understand Deirdre's problem.

"Don't you worry about me," Deirdre said. "I know what I'm doing. I won't get into any trouble."

Kessa felt limp with hopelessness, remembering her own resistance to help. "Sure you do," she mumbled. "I'll see you later. 'Bye"

She sat down in front of her locker, thinking back: how she'd fought everything—her parents, her doctors, food. She'd fought eating so much that a pump had to do it for her. And how often had she said *Don't worry about me! I'll be okay! Why do you want me to be fat?*

Kessa got out of bed, grabbed the pole that supported the infusion pump and jerked it around sharply, inadvertently pulling the line near the point where it was stitched to her chest.

"Ow! Damnit!" She pressed the area around the stitches, noticing a trickle of blood staining her robe. She pulled the machine hard as she walked rapidly to the nurses' station. When she was within five feet of the nurses, she yelled, "I'm bleeding!"

Two of the nurses, writing on charts, looked up and walked over to her together. One of them reached toward Kessa's chest, seemed to adjust something, and then looked at this skeleton of a patient.

"How did you manage to open the juncture in your line?" she asked.

Kessa looked down, saw the entire front of her robe covered with blood, and fainted.

Both of the nurses grabbed her before she could hit the ground. They sat her down on the floor with her back against the waist-high partition counter and elevated her knees.

Kessa moved her head slowly, then opened her eyes without focusing them.

"Kessa, you're not in any danger," one of the nurses said reassuringly. "The line opened and you lost some blood, but it looks a lot worse than it is. We've closed the line now and everything's okay. We just have to clean you up and change all the tubing." They helped her up and practically carried her back to the room.

Kessa forgot to be angry. So many people taking care of her was overpowering yet comforting at the same time.

Sandy Sherman's phone rang.

"Hello, Sandy. Gerry Donaldson. You may get a complaint from your rather agitated patient, Miss Dietrich. She's all right, but she scared herself. Somehow her line became undone. She lost an insignificant amount of blood, but it looked bad on the front of her robe. In her typical fashion, she may accuse you of having put her in an unsafe hospital. I know how these kinds of patients can upset everyone around them, so watch out for her call."

"Thanks for the warning, Gerry, but I think I'll head off her call with one of my own."

Kessa watched as the resident and nurse put on sterile surgical gloves, clamped and disconnected the transparent plastic tubing from her chest to the infusion pump, then attached new tubing and adjusted the valves to restart the dreaded fluids.

"Sorry I made a mess of this stuff."

The resident was not much older than his late twenties. Lean and muscular, with dark straight hair, he had deep-set eyes that looked intently from the lines, their junctures, and the bandage on Kessa's chest to the counter on the infusion pump and, finally, to Kessa's face.

"Everything looks fine now," he said, his voice a serious near-whisper. "Try not to pull at the line. It's not built to take too much tension."

She smiled because he seemed to be taking her pump so seriously. "I'm afraid I'm not, either."

"What do you mean?"

"I'm not built to take much tension, either."

He stared at her for a moment. "You'll be all right now." He smiled, nodded his head, straightened up, and walked quickly out of the room.

"Show off!" exclaimed Gail, one of the nurses, as soon as he was out of earshot.

Kessa looked perplexed.

"He's into being Dr. Kildare. It's his second year of residency. They think they become next to God by the end

of this year." Gail shook her head and went on. "I've
watched fifteen classes of them rotated through this hospital. They come back five or six years later and they're
human again, and a lot more grown-up. The young ones are
the worst. Working with them means wiping their noses and
propping up their overinflated egos." She winked
conspiratorially.

Kessa liked Gail. She was quiet and confident and sooth-
ing and seemed a whole lot smarter than the show-off
resident. Kessa decided that she would like to be like Gail
when she got older.

"Gail, how come I feel so young here?"

The nurse smiled warmly. She was about five foot eight,
with broad shoulders and a large bust—a little bit heavy,
but not fat at all. Just large. She was pretty, too, and always
wore her shoulder-length platinum hair pulled over the side
with a sparkly barrette. Gail always looked self-assured no
matter what she was doing. Kessa wanted to acquire that
confidence. How much she admired people who were
stronger than she was. She often sought out Gail during the
day, offering to help her with whatever tasks she was per-
mitted to. Gail was aware of Kessa's admiration, as well as
her precarious emotional state, and offered Kessa approval
whenever she felt it was appropriate.

"I think all of us feel a little younger when people take
care of us," she replied. "Maybe you've been trying to be too
old, pushing yourself too far."

"Maybe."

"Maybe you could stop trying so hard, Kessa. Even here
in the hospital you're always trying to be so helpful. You try
to learn how to be a nurse while you're still the patient. You
always push so hard in so many directions that I worry you
might burn yourself out one way or another."

"I'm always afraid. Sometimes I don't know what I'm

afraid of, but when I do, it's a fear of falling behind, of everybody getting ahead of me. I just feel like if I'm not careful, I'll become nothing. Invisible."

Gail leaned over the bed, brushed Kessa's bangs off her face, and smiled at her with real affection. "I guess you want to be shiny, huh?"

Kessa nodded.

"If that's *what* you want, I wonder *who* you want to share it with."

"What do you mean?"

"You sound so lonely. You're full of 'whats,' but no 'who.' It seems like there's no one in your life, no one that you feel touched by."

Tears started to trickle down Kessa's cheeks.

Gail touched a tear stain gently. "Get some rest, Kessa. Take a break from all this. I'll see you later."

After Gail left the room, Kessa wanted to call out to her, to ask her not to go, to stay with her, to cuddle her, to tell her she'd be all right, that she wouldn't get too fat. That she wouldn't become invisible.

Kessa was late. As soon as she entered the gym, she immediately began to look for Deirdre. Most of the girls had gathered around the piece of gymnastic apparatus they'd be working with. Deirdre was at the parallel bars, flexing and stretching before her mount. Kessa looked down at her own arms, comparing them with Deirdre's. For a moment she felt a deep twinge of envy for Deirdre's long, bony limbs. She wished she were tall like Deirdre—then she could have longer arms, which would look thinner anyway. She pinched one arm, watching her flesh turn white, then pink. *Fat*.

Suddenly, she noticed that her teacher and several of the girls had clustered around someone who had fallen to the mat. The teacher was examining the girl's wrists, commenting that one of them might be sprained.

As Deirdre was helped to her feet, she saw Kessa watching. She shrugged her shoulders apologetically and mumbled, "Weak wrists," then walked off with the teacher to the nurse's office.

Kessa looked down at her arm again. It was still pink from where she'd pinched it. Still *fat*.

Chapter
14

"Why does she make me so mad?"

Sherman shrugged his shoulders. "I don't know."

That was no answer. It pissed her off. "What do you mean, 'I don't know'?" She imitated his voice. "You're always offering me answers and explanations for things I ask you about. Why are you so puzzled all of a sudden?"

"I think you have to figure this one out, and while you're at it, try to figure out why you're throwing such a temper tantrum when I say I don't know."

"I guess I expect you to always know the answer," Kessa said slowly. "My parents always told me I could do what I wanted, that I could figure out anything I had to . . . and I couldn't. But I never could say that. It was unthinkable to say 'I can't.' "

Sherman smiled at her. That got Kessa confused. Why would he approve of her complaining? "What are you smiling about? I think the whole thing stinks, and you're still not answering my question about being so mad at Deirdre."

"I'm smiling because you have really learned to think the

unthinkable and demand the undemandable with me.
You're so mad at me for asking you to figure it out yourself.
And I think that's terrific. I think you're learning how to say
'help' and you're furious at Deirdre because she's in trouble
and denying it to you—just like you denied you were in
trouble while you were losing weight."

"Was I really as much trouble to you as Deirdre is to
me?"

Sandy's smile widened. "If I tell you that you were
trouble you might apologize, and you know how I object to
your apologizing for your personality—or your existence."

Kessa bit her lip. "It sounds like you don't want me to be
very nice."

He nodded. "That's right. Not ever as nice as when I met
you. Nobody should have to be that nice."

"Why not?"

"If you have to be nice when you don't want to, you will
be 'angrily nice.' If that happens often enough, you store up
lots of anger and one day blow up over nothing. Then you'll
be ashamed for having blown up and go back to angrily nice
until the next cycle and the next blow-up."

"But nobody likes someone who isn't nice. I don't want
everybody to hate me."

"In order to lie to everyone else, you've got to lie to
yourself. So if you have to act a role with everyone, you have
to fool yourself to make it work. And when you fool yourself,
you end up being out of touch with yourself and you might
think you're too fat when you're actually too thin. Deirdre's
out of touch with herself. She's skinny and losing weight and
lying—first to herself and second to you. *You* get very mad
when you are lied to. So even though Deirdre's *nice*, it
doesn't work. You get mad at her niceness!"

Kessa sat silently, an anxious look on her face.

"What's the matter, Kessa?"

"How do I know when . . . I'm not nice enough, when *you* won't want to be bothered with me, when *nobody* will? How can I tell?"

"You can't."

"But that's scary."

"It is."

"I don't like not being able to know what will happen."

"Nobody does."

"But if we can't tell, then don't we have to be very careful?"

"Kessa, somewhere between being totally absorbed in somebody else and totally self-centered lies some reasonable approach to people. Uncertainty and a willingness to take risks is something we all have to learn how to tolerate."

She frowned. "I hate taking risks."

"You took one today when you yelled at me."

"That was different."

"How?"

"Because I forgot to be scared."

Kessa stared at the phone. She wanted to talk to Deirdre the way Sandy had spoken to her that afternoon, wanted to get past Deirdre's niceness. With a shaky hand, she dialed the number, and after a few rings, Deirdre answered in a friendly voice.

"Hello, McGuire residence."

"Is that you Deirdre?"

"Kessa?"

"You sound like the maid."

"We don't have a maid. How are you?"

"I called to see how your wrist is."

"Oh, it's fine."

"It didn't look so fine when you left the gym."

"Hey, don't worry about it. It's really all right."

Kessa was starting to get annoyed. "What did the doctor say?"

"Oh, it's just a sprain."

"That must hurt."

"Only a little."

"I'm sorry you sprained your wrist, Deirdre."

"It's not your fault."

"I don't think that it's my fault. It's just an expression of sympathy on my part." Kessa's jaw was clenched, she was so tense. She'd listened very carefully to Deirdre's responses, and they were driving her nuts.

"C'mon, Kessa. It's not serious. It's just a sprain."

"It's not serious for me to express sympathy either unless it upsets you to hear anything."

Sure. Kessa covered the mouthpiece and mouthed an "I bet!" to her room. Then she said aloud, "Deirdre, I think it upsets you if somebody is nice to you, if someone compliments you or expresses sympathy or something. Because every time I do any of those things, you squirm out of it as if I didn't say it or I shouldn't have said it. It makes me feel dumb."

"I don't want to hurt your feelings. I mean, if I thought something would hurt your—"

"Wait a minute. I know how that ends, but I wish you wouldn't try so hard."

"I don't know what you mean."

"Never mind. I hope your wrist feels better, and I'll see you tomorrow in gym."

"Are you sure you're not mad at me?"

Kessa tried to tease her. "Even if I were, it wouldn't be serious. 'Bye."

Kessa hung up, then talked to the silent telephone. It was

easier to talk when no one was listening.

"Poor Deirdre. I was right. She's so nice she makes me sick. She's never sure where she stands.

"And God knows, I've been there often enough."

Deirdre had found the conversation unsettling. Kessa just knew too much about her behavior, and it made her confused and angry. But she still wanted to be friends.

She walked to the kitchen, downed an entire box of corn flakes with a quart of skim milk, walked to the bathroom, threw it all up, and sat down to do her homework.

Grace called Kessa and Harold to dinner. Kessa noticed that her father's before-dinner drinks had become smaller again and he wasn't quite so cranky all the time.

"I hear you have a new friend, Francesca. Is she somebody from school?"

Kessa winced at the use of Francesca, but decided to ignore it. She wanted her father to stay in a good mood.

"Yes, Daddy. We're in gymnastics together."

Harold grew uneasy. Was this participation in gymnastics going to turn into another obsession like her dancing had been? He wondered about how exercise could lead to weight loss as he tried to watch Kessa eat without looking directly at her.

Kessa sensed her father's eyes upon her plate and wondered how long it would continue. Sometimes she ate less when she knew he was watching her.

"So this new friend of yours, Deirdre, is she your age?"

"I think so. It's funny. I just haven't asked her."

"Your mother said Deirdre's awfully skinny. Do you think she has anorexia?"

Harold had posed the question perfectly. They'd all been waiting for it to come out, so it was a relief to be able to answer. And Kessa was secretly flattered that her father was asking *her* opinion about such a touchy subject.

"Yes, Daddy, *I* think she has it. But *she* doesn't."

That was the answer Hal wanted to hear. There was nothing conspiratorial in it at all.

"Does it hurt your own progress to be friends with her?"

The word *progress* irritated Kessa.

"No, I don't think it hurts my *progress*," she said sarcastically. The moment of understanding melted away.

Hal immediately got defensive. "You know what I mean. We've all just been through hell with this—"

"*You've* all just been through hell. *I'm* still *in* hell!"

Hal guiltily met his wife's eyes. "We just don't want you feeling worse. That's all, Kessa."

He called her Kessa. Well, that was "progress." Back to neutral territory. "I don't know if Deirdre's anorectic, but I won't not be her friend if she is," Kessa said. "I would hate it if everyone backed away from me when I was in the most trouble."

"Didn't they?"

"No. I did the backing away. Nobody could get near me, and that's what she's doing. I'm not going to let her slip away the way I did...and am still tempted to do sometimes."

Harold got the message. "Then she's welcome here."

"Thanks, Daddy."

Harold took a glass of brandy and the newspaper into the living room after dinner, thinking about his daughter's "progress" and her reaction to that word. She *was* getting better, and he was *trying* to understand her complicated moods. He hoped he was getting better at talking to her. There'd been a time when he hadn't known what to say at all.

* * *

Harold stared out the window at Central Park while his wife poured him a drink. "How do you think she's doing in that hospital?" he asked.

"I think she's doing all right." The glass overflowed. Grace snatched a sponge from the sink and wiped the spill.

Harold hadn't noticed her clumsiness. "What do you mean?"

"I don't know how to tell if she's doing all right or improving. This isn't like summer camp. I don't know what it will take to get her over this. I'm tired of feeling like this is all my fault and that the decision to hospitalize her is my sole responsibility. What else do you want from me?"

Harold was about to defend himself when he noticed that she was crying quietly. He turned away and walked to one of the tall windows overlooking Central Park. For an instant he wanted to forget everything and simply enjoy the view, pretend his daughter was still the best little girl in the world.

"What are we supposed to do about this? How are we supposed to know what's best for her? How can we tell if she's getting better—whatever the hell that means? I've never felt so lost or helpless in my life. When something goes wrong with the business, at least I know what steps to take," Hal confessed. "If something breaks in the house, I know how to fix it. When a difficult customer comes in, I know how to talk to him. I don't even know how to talk to my kid. I don't know whether what I say will cause her to eat more or starve to death, whether she'll smile or frown, whether she'll feel like I love her or hate her. Part of the time I feel sorry for her and part of the time I want to—I'm furious at her. So I was hoping you or the doctors or *somebody* would know . . . could tell what's better or worse for her. Suddenly I see her as a crazy person. I guess a crazy person is someone who's hopelessly impossible to understand. . . ." His voice faltered as tears welled up in his eyes. "I don't want my daughter to be crazy!"

Grace walked over to him and gently put her hand on the back of his neck. She knew he couldn't bear for her to see his tears, so she stayed in that position with him.

"I think that we're both a little lost right now," she said softly, "but I can handle it if I know it's both of us—not just me." *I just couldn't bear the burden of complete blame and responsibility anymore*, she added to herself.

"It's both of us, Grace. I can promise you that."

"If that's so, then I would like to ask you for a huge favor."

He turned around to face her. "What is it?"

"When she calls us from the hospital, I want you to answer the phone and deal with her for a while. It's got me beat. No matter what I say, it's wrong. She's so angry. I just don't want to talk to her for a while."

"What will you do if she calls when I'm at work?"

He was right. Grace felt trapped.

"I guess I really can't hide from my own child," she said ruefully. "Well, when you're home, you can answer the phone. At least I'll know I'm not on all the time."

The streetlights in Central Park twinkled in the dark. Harold put down his empty brandy snifter and picked up the newspaper.

Chapter
15

Sandy Sherman played with a pen while Kessa talked.

"Whenever my father makes me mad, it feels like six months ago. I feel fat right away. I want to lose weight."

Sandy didn't respond immediately.

"Why are you playing with that pen? You never take notes anyway."

He laughed. "You think I should take notes?"

"Sometimes you make me as mad as my father."

"Do you want to lose weight when you get mad at me, too?"

"If I have to fight with you, who can I talk to?"

"All right, I won't be a wise guy. Let's back up a bit. Remember when you said that if you weren't 'starving skinny' you were afraid you wouldn't be anything?"

"Yeah."

"Why did we decide you felt that way?"

"You decided that I had no other way of fighting back. As you put it, of being assertive." She put a heavy emphasis on the last word.

"Do you think you'll skip a meal after our session?"

"No. Why do you ask?"

"I didn't think you would. You've become too much of a fighter for that."

"You mean I was starving instead of fighting?"

"Starving is your imaginary way of dealing with the world."

"What do you mean, 'imaginary'?"

"When you've lost weight, it's made you feel like you've done something to somebody, settled a score, defeated them."

"You make it sound like I'm some bitch! I wanted to talk to you about that last week." Her voice sounded shaky. "I just don't think I'm as mean as you make me out to be."

"I never thought of you as mean. I've thought of you as helpless."

"But that's even worse! I've never been helpless in all my life. I've always gotten the grades. I've had friends. I've managed my life and all the people in it perfectly . . . and you call me helpless!"

"Have you 'managed' people within all your relationships?"

"Yes, and I think that I've done a pretty good job, too. I don't know how you can call that helpless."

"When you started losing weight and everyone was critical of you for being too thin, you were no longer able to manage them. Since your relationships with your friends *and* your parents were managerial in style, when you were no longer in charge because your weight and appearance declared you incompetent, then you were helpless. The more helpless you became, the less you could manage those around you, so the more you relied on losing weight for a sense of control over your life. You weren't relying on any sort of intimacy—you were more the manager. And when you were demoted, you withdrew from others. It seems to me that you think that you've got to regain your management of others in order to feel adequate and safe. Otherwise, when you feel helpless, you'll turn back to weight control as a substitute for managing others."

Kessa sat quietly for a few minutes, mulling over Sandy's sermon. She knew that much of what he'd said made perfect sense, though she didn't want to admit it, but she also worried that his comments might be masking a scathing condemnation. And she couldn't bear that from someone she trusted so intimately.

"So what are you saying I should be doing that I'm not?"

"You might stop living your life like a one-way mirror. It's as if you can look into everyone else but no one is able to look back."

"But I'm trying that with Deirdre and she's worse than a mirror. She's a brick wall."

"Deirdre's going to be tougher than most people because she's so much like you. You do have an advantage, though."

"What's that?"

"You know who she is because you're so similar. You could tell Deirdre what you know about her without getting angry at her."

"How do *you* know so much about who I am? Are you like me?"

"Maybe."

They smiled at each other. Sandy was proud of Kessa. She really was turning into a fighter.

The bell rang. Gymnastics was over and it was time for lunch. Deirdre looked at her watch as she hurried into the locker room.

"Kessa, I've got to get going."

"Why?"

"I've got an appointment . . . I'll see you later."

"Let's have lunch first."

"Oh no! I've got to go."

"Bullshit! You're just scared to eat with me."

"Hey, no way! I'm just busy."

"I remember when I was scared to eat with people. I still am sometimes."

"Is this a dare or something?"

"I want you to eat with me."

"All right. I can handle it," she said, but her empty stomach was churning with anxiety.

They walked out onto Lexington Avenue, where bakeries, coffee shops, delis, and pizza parlors competed for the dollars of hungry New Yorkers.

"Pick a place, Kessa," Deirdre said nervously.

She pointed downtown. "They have good pizza two blocks that way."

"Fine."

"It's tiny and a little dumpy, but the pizza's the best."

Gino and Gina's had squeezed four tiny tables into a space barely larger than a walk-in closet. Take-out boxes were piled a dozen high to the low ceiling on either side of the ovens, and take-out customers waited patiently at the long Formica counter.

Deirdre felt a little claustrophobic. "You weren't kidding about dumpy. I hope the food tastes better than this place looks."

"It does," Kessa said smugly.

Kessa ordered two slices plain. Deirdre ordered three slices with pepperoni and mushrooms, and she wolfed them down before Kessa had started her second piece.

"You were right," she said with a smile. "This stuff's the best."

"Glad you appreciated it. I'm full."

Deirdre scanned the tiny place. Three other tables, a long counter, and Gino and Gina busy at the pizza ovens. There was no ladies' room to be seen. She went very pale.

"Hey, haven't they got a bathroom here?"

"No. They've probably got one hidden away that they use, but they won't admit it to the customer."

Deirdre felt tricked. This had been a setup. "You knew this place had no bathroom," she said, trying to keep the anger out of her voice, "and everyone has to go after lunch, Kessa."

"Yeah, we should have gone back at school."

"Let's go back to school then!"

"What's the emergency? It's only two blocks away. We can wait a few minutes. We're on the same schedule, and I'm not going in my pants."

"Everybody's different! Are you coming?"

"All right. You act like I'm messing you up or something."

Deirdre hurried out into the cold. Kessa practically had to run to keep up with her.

"C'mon, Kessa. Can't you walk faster?"

Deirdre raced up the stairs at Hinkley and didn't slow down till she reached the door to the ladies' room. She stopped and looked back nervously at Kessa, who had a stitch in her side from running after eating.

"I'll go first. You wait here."

"Deirdre, there are four toilets in there. Why should I wait here?"

"I don't think that pizza was so good after all. I think I'm going to throw up. You don't want to be around for that, do you?"

"You're such a bullshit artist! You knew when you were eating that you were going to throw up! You must eat plenty too, the way you swallowed those slices. You're not sick from that pizza. You're a vomiter! Why don't we stand out here for forty-five minutes and see if the urge passes."

"I'm going in!" Deirdre pushed the door open.

"And I'm going to listen to you stick your fingers down your throat . . . and I'm going to hear the whole performance!" She pushed in after her friend.

"What the hell do you want from me anyway?" Deirdre shouted.

"Right now, I'd like to screw a cork in your mouth!"

"You're horrible!"

"No, damnit! I'm not horrible. I'm just like you, that's all, and I hate what you do."

Deirdre's eyes welled up with tears. "What do you want from me?" she repeated.

"I want you to not throw up!"

"I have to!"

"Why?"

"I don't know!" She began to tremble.

"You won't get fat, Deirdre." Kessa tried to reassure.

"I will! I will!" Deirdre was sobbing hysterically as she edged closer to the toilet stall. "I will! You have to let me!"

Kessa stood paralyzed for a minute, taken aback by the authority Deirdre had conferred upon her. She didn't want that authority. God, how well she remembered her own struggles. She too began to cry—for Deirdre, for herself, for all the hurt in the world. She tried to give Deirdre a hug, but Deirdre was intent on only one thing. In one swift motion she pushed Kessa to one side, fought for a position over the toilet, and threw up before Kessa had a chance to stop her.

Kessa ran out of the bathroom, still in tears. She paced down the hallway, glad that all the rest of the students were still at lunch. She didn't know whether she was more angry at or more scared of Deirdre.

Deirdre washed her face and drank some water, then sat

down on the bathroom floor, now afraid of what Kessa might think.

After fifteen minutes, Deirdre still had not come out. Kessa became worried. What if she's fainted or something?

"Deirdre?" she called out as she pushed open the door.

Deirdre was huddled in the corner. "Yeah?" she said between hiccups.

"Are you all right?"

"No."

"What do you mean?"

"How could someone like me be all right? I'm not even *half* right," she said sarcastically.

Kessa began to cry again. Deirdre's response was to hunch down even further on the cold bathroom floor. She didn't see Kessa's crying as a sign of sympathy; she was sure, with her own tortured logic, that Kessa was somehow condemning her.

"Why do you want to look like that? Why do you want to do that stuff?" Kessa blurted.

Deirdre's eyes glazed over. "I'm not talking to you about the way I look."

Kessa looked at the woebegone girl's nearly skeletal arms and legs, conflicting feelings of jealousy, anger, and frustration bombarding her at once. She couldn't fight Deirdre—she needed her energy for her *own* survival.

"Do you want to be friends anyway?" she ventured, resigned to whatever bizarre behavior she knew she'd encounter.

Deirdre tried to smile. "I think we are already."

Kessa stared at the floor. "Sometimes we'll fight, I guess."

"I don't want to."

"Too bad." Kessa smiled. "We're stuck with that."

"What does your shrink say about all this?"

"You're not going to like this," she said, trying to tease her friend. "He says that we don't know how to feel secure and that we're 'skinny junkies.' He says we're killing ourselves to try to feel a sense of self. I get embarrassed when he says that. It makes me ashamed."

"Do you think he's right?"

"I don't know. I want *somebody* to be right about me, but I hate hearing stuff that basically just means I don't know what I'm doing."

"How can anybody be right about what's good for anybody else?" Deirdre asked cynically. "I mean, he's not in your skin . . . or mine."

"Yeah, sometimes I think that. Other times I know I'm fooling myself, and the truth really is I don't know what I'm doing and I actually pray that he's right because I need somebody else to be right when I'm lost. Even if he's not right, I want to *pretend* he's right, so I don't feel so alone. Other times I hate him and think he's got a shitload of nerve telling me about myself."

"Why don't you get rid of him? I mean, really, get rid of this guy then. Be your own person. He's just on a power trip with your head."

"The last time I was on my own, I nearly died."

"C'mon, Kessa. You've got to do it yourself!"

"Do what myself."

"Um . . . do *everything* yourself."

"Why?"

"So you're your own person."

"I'm tired of being my own person. It stinks. And besides, I don't know who I am anyway. Do you?"

"No, but when I've found out, it will be *me* who makes me what I am!"

"Did you give birth to yourself?"

Deirdre looked annoyed. "No, but sometimes it feels like

I did. I've always been in charge of myself . . . and *them*, all of them."

"Didn't you ever wish you weren't?"

"I don't even try to wish for what I can't have."

"You know, sometimes you sound like some tough street kid. Except I know I'm kidding myself when I listen to *you* kid yourself."

"Now you're doing to me what your shrink does to you. You're telling me what's best for me, and I don't like it."

Kessa backed off. "Well, I'm going to keep letting someone else make me what I become, while you do it for yourself. I'm too tired of doing it for myself." *For now, anyway*, she added to herself.

She'd misplaced her keys again, so Kessa rang the front doorbell.

Grace opened it, looking anxious and relieved at the same time. "Where have you been Fr—Kessa? It's nearly six o'clock."

"Watching Deirdre barf," Kessa responded sullenly.

"What? What are you talking about?"

"Oh, Mom. I like her, but she's even worse than I was. But I'm staying her friend and I don't want to talk about it."

Why, Grace wondered, *of all the girls at school, did her daughter have to befriend another anorectic?* It was just too complicated. "Are you ready for dinner?"

"Yeah, I'm *ready* for it."

"Well, don't make it sound like such an ordeal!"

"I wouldn't make it sound like an ordeal if you wouldn't keep making it sound like a test. You sit there and watch me like a hawk at every meal. I'm tired of proving things to you and Dad."

"So do all of your friends have anorexia?"

"Every last one of them. Now, what's for dinner?"

Chapter
16

Kessa looked at Sherman suspiciously. She remembered all of Deirdre's accusations and wondered whether listening to him amounted to some sort of cowardice.

"You're pretty quiet today, Kessa. What's that about?"

"I don't know," she said sullenly.

"Are you mad at somebody?"

"Why did you say that?"

"Because you look angry."

Kessa knew she did look angry, but she wasn't about to give in. "What makes you think you can always tell what I'm thinking?"

"I can never tell you what you're thinking. I can only watch you and listen to you."

"So does that tell you what I'm thinking?"

"Sometimes."

"How do you know you're right?"

"It looks like I'm not looking too *right* to you today, hm?"

"I just get annoyed, and sometimes I think you're trying to rip me off."

"In what way?"

" 'Cause you're not always right."

"What are we really talking about here?"

"What I said we were."

Sandy leaned back in his chair. "It seems that you came in here feeling pushed around by me before I even said anything."

"Maybe I did."

"Well, since you feel pushed around and I haven't seen you for four days, I probably haven't done anything to you. So I wonder why you're so angry with me."

"I just don't know how much I'm supposed to depend on you. It makes me feel creepy."

"How much you depend on me is up to you." What had triggered this? he wondered. "When it makes you feel creepy, don't."

"But I feel scared when I can't trust you."

"What happens that makes you not want to trust?"

"Sometimes it makes me feel weak. Why can't I depend on myself? Why do I need to talk to you?"

"Trust and weakness are two different things. I think you're mixing them up."

"Dependency is a weakness," Kessa said matter-of-factly. "It means you're not self-sufficient."

"Dependency is an arrangement that exists in nature, friendship, business, and families."

Sandy always sounded so calm and logical. "Well," Kessa admitted, trying not to pout, "sometimes the arrangement stinks."

"It stinks when one party is doing all the giving and the other is doing all of the getting."

"Why do I feel like I'm doing all of the giving even though I know I'm not?"

"How much of the getting are you doing?"

"As much as I choose to," Kessa said defensively.

"And how much is that?"

Kessa couldn't answer him directly. "Why does it feel so icky for me to 'get'?"

"Because you learned it was icky."

"Nobody told me it was bad."

"Maybe nobody told you it was okay, either."

"Oh sure, who's gonna tell me? People don't tell people that kind of stuff," Kessa remarked sarcastically.

"Right now you're telling me how annoyed with me you are, without stating it in a straightforward manner."

He was right. "But how would somebody tell me that it's bad to receive anything?"

"They might praise you for independence, for example, or tell you that there's nothing you can't do, tell you that you shouldn't care about what anybody else thinks. They might even tell you that you're smarter than they are, and can probably solve your own problems better than they can— even when you were very young."

"Is that why I believe all that stuff you just said?"

"Oh, do you?" He smiled at her. "Just coincidence, I guess."

"No, c'mon. How did you know that?"

"Because you care so much about what everybody thinks. You're afraid that you'll never solve any of your own problems, and you don't think that you're as smart as anybody else . . . who's smart."

"But that's the opposite—"

"If you're told what you *should* be but not helped to *become* it, you don't get there. And it makes you ashamed for failing to. When a person you depend on keeps telling you that it's time to 'move on,' 'to grow up,' it makes you feel that who you are now is inadequate or uninteresting."

"But you can't always tell people that they're great when

they're not," she protested, "or they might just suck their thumbs for the rest of their lives and think that's terrific."

"No, and you can't become too skinny to avoid becoming too fat either."

"Oh, you're always just full of tricks." Kessa made a teasing face. She was actually beginning to enjoy challenging Sandy in their sessions, and she was learning not to take everything so seriously. It was hard—it was torture sometimes—but once in a while Kessa actually *felt* her progress, like it was some tangible thing, almost as if she had broken her arm and she could feel the bones fusing together in a new sort of strength. "I'm not mad at you anymore. I guess I'll go have lunch now."

"Lunch?" Sandy scratched his beard and peered over his glasses in a mock inspection. "It's nearly four o'clock."

"Yeah." She couldn't meet his gaze. She looked down. "I was too mad at you to eat until now."

"So when you get made at *me*, you punish *yourself*."

"Well, it's easier."

Sandy laughed. "It's easier for *me*, too! Thanks Kessa. You're a good sport."

"Maybe next time I could starve you instead of me." The thought of rumply Sandy Sherman starving was too funny. Kessa had to laugh too.

"Good idea," he shouted after her.

Kessa was idly walking up Madison Avenue when she notice a familiar figure striding ahead of her—a nearly five-foot ten-inch girl with thinning shoulder-length hair. The jacket she was wearing seemed about ten sizes too big, and her legs were like sticks, adrift in baggy pants.

Staying a few paces behind, she studied Deirdre's right and left profile as she looked both ways before crossing the intersection. She thought about how Deirdre's little upturned nose, sharply etched jaw, and gaunt cheekbones might be just what some fashion photographer was looking for. But what would he do about the bony ridge over each eye? They'd probably just cover that with bangs, she thought. There was an excuse for everything.

Kessa never wanted to talk to anybody after a session with Sherman. It was her private time, when she replayed the afternoon's comments and digested their conversation. And the last person she could share that with was Deirdre.

She hurried into a coffee shop, hoping that Deirdre wouldn't turn around and see her. She looked at the clock above the counter. 4:08. This was going to be tough. If she ate now, she reasoned, she wouldn't be hungry for dinner at six, and her parents would drive her crazy. So she should eat something light but not filling. She ordered a bran muffin without butter and black coffee, feeling a pang of disappointment when the waiter didn't ask her if that was all she wanted. When she'd been as skinny as Deirdre and made a similar order, the waiters invariably looked concerned or upset with her. That response meant she was virtuously, even shockingly, skinny. The only thing that really ever bothered her was when kids her age would point at her and elbow each other, whispering loudly, "Anorexia, look. Yech!" Why did they have to make fun of her? Why were they so mean about her appearance?

"Miss? Did you say butter?" The waiter jolted her back to reality.

"No. No butter."

Maybe she was still skinny enough. . . .

She ate half of the muffin and finished the coffee. Timidly, she approached the cashier, almost hoping that the waiter would pursue her about her unfinished portion. But when she looked over her shoulder, she saw him tilting her plate into the garbage and wiping a few crumbs off the counter. It was as if his rag had totally obliterated her presence.

Kessa tried not to focus on depressing thoughts as she buttoned her jacket before she walked out into the darkening afternoon. *I think about myself all the time*, she realized with a start as she headed over to Eighty-sixth Street to catch the crosstown bus. *I've got to focus more on other people*. She eyed them hurrying past her, intent on getting home after a day's work. She noticed an awful lot of weary men with executive-type coats thrown over their dark business suits. They all had briefcases. In fact, they all seemed stamped out of sort of the same mold. And there weren't as many women who looked so businesslike and serious. She wondered where most of the women were on Manhattan's Upper East Side at five in the afternoon.

And then she wondered where she would be at five in the afternoon when she grew up. She laughed ironically at herself when she thought of that phrase. It was one she hadn't used in years.

"When I grow up—that'll be never!"

"Excuse me?" a man with a leather attaché case inquired politely.

"Oh! I'm sorry. I thought you were someone else."

He nodded understandingly and continued on his way.

Maybe he's a lawyer, she thought. Or a banker. Daddy said once that they're always supposed to wear navy or gray suits, not brown or any other colors. That's pretty dumb. I wonder what I'll have to wear to work. *If* I go to work.

When Kessa walked into her lobby she saw a large man standing in front of the elevator door. It was her father, and he was wearing a brown suit. She felt a stab of pride. He was the president of his very own company and he could wear whatever color of suit he wanted. She watched him surreptitiously for a few moments, just as she'd watched Deirdre earlier.

Harold, a heavy-set man in his mid-fifties, broad-shouldered, balding, with a thick old-fashioned moustache, still retained the build of a laborer, believing the maxim "If you want something done right, you've got to do it yourself" applied to his business as much as any other. He was a self-made man who had begun as an apprentice in the tool and die business and, nearly forty years later, owned the second largest die manufacturing company in lower Manhattan. That, of course, didn't stop him from moving heavy stock around during the day. Kessa heard him complain frequently that he could be the largest maker of machine parts except that the ever-inflating prices of property in Soho, the trendy area of art galleries and boutiques in lower Manhattan, prevented him from expanding.

Observing him unnoticed, Kessa felt a warmth for him that had been missing for quite a while. He was a man who, as her mother said, "struggled to succeed." Kessa realized she finally understood what that meant. She wondered what it would be like to have enough confidence to start up a business and go after success. She wanted so badly to ask him if he had ever been scared, or doubted himself . . . or if he was always scared. No, she decided she didn't want to know. If her father admitted he got scared, it was better not to know.

"Hi, Daddy."

He turned around, his weariness evident. Harold Dietrich worked too hard. He smiled at his daughter. "Hi, honey." Then he looked at his watch. "Isn't it a little late for you to be getting home from school?"

"I had an appointment at Dr. Sherman's."

"Oh."

"How was your day?"

Hal was surprised by the question. Kessa had never asked him about work before. "You don't want to know."

"If I didn't want to know, then I wouldn't have asked," Kessa pressed him.

"It was the same as usual."

"Is that good?"

"Okay."

Obviously, Kessa thought, he doesn't want to talk about it. It must be important to him to keep his day a secret. The other men, in their gray suits, must have secret days too. Men had always seemed so alien to her. She didn't understand them at all. Even the boys in her school began to seem strange to her as they got older. They started to wear blue blazers, talk seriously about colleges and summer internships and financial planning, and girls. Soon they would exchange their blue blazers for gray suits and she would lose contact with them for good.

Charles greeted them and they rode the elevator up in silence. Kessa's warm regard for her father was rapidly disappearing. He just didn't want to talk to her because she wasn't important enough for him to confide in. Her father was just a tired inspector who wanted to know why she was late and monitored every bite she took. He was never really interested, just polite, almost as if they were strangers at a party. She'd never seen the reflection of a pretty girl in his eyes. Maybe he meant well.

Maybe.

Kessa looked at her hideous, deformed body in the mirror. She was a huge fat blimp. All she could see were hips and thighs. Like her father, she was now an inspector of the Kessa Dietrich body. And it was a faulty model, no refund, no exchanges. She remembered a scene from the movie *West*

Side Story and wondered what it would be like to stand in front of the mirror as Maria had done . . . and feel pretty. All she could see now were lines and shapes, not a person. Certainly not a *pretty* person.

"Kessa!" Grace called. "Dinner's ready."

At least her mother always called her by her real name now. "I'm coming—just changing. Be ready in a sec!" She'd cope with dinner as well as her mother coped with her name. In other words, not very well at all. It suddenly seemed like a very small victory to have her mother call her Kessa. Why did everything feel like a contest, a contest where no one was ever the winner?

Hal was more talkative at the table than he'd been in the lobby. "What sort of day did you have, Kessa?"

"It was okay."

"How was therapy?"

She always hated that question and never answered it. Even if therapy had no other value, it was worth continuing just so it could be something she did entirely her own.

"Everything's okay, Daddy." Her day could be as much of a secret as his.

Grace looked on timidly. Her daughter still seemed too thin to her, and she knew from her repeated attempts at reassurance that Kessa still thought of herself as fat. Grace almost thought of her daughter as a ticking time-bomb that might go off any day. Except the bomb wouldn't explode. It would just stop eating.

Grace's fears were so transparent, Kessa sometimes thought that they only tempted her to torment her mother. When Kessa was angry, she would eat less at the table. At dinnertime Kessa felt the most powerful, most angry, and most persecuted.

Harold cleared his throat. "These are good lamb chops, aren't they?"

"I don't know, Daddy. I'm having fish."

"Grace, since when are we having two separate meals?"

"What's the difference, Hal? As long as we're all enjoying dinner."

Harold felt tricked. Grace worried about an argument. And Kessa braced herself, sullenly waiting for the next round.

"Kessa looks good, doesn't she, Grace?"

Kessa cringed.

"Everyone here looks good, Hal."

Kessa glanced instinctively at her own arms. *Fat.* Grace noticed; Harold didn't. Time to change the subject.

"How was your day, Hal?"

"It was all right. You know, I think my outfit is getting bigger than Schumacher's—and he's the oldest tool and die maker in the East."

"That's exciting, Hal. What will you do next?"

"Sell the whole thing to a conglomerate and retire in a few years, I hope."

"What will we do when you retire?" Kessa momentarily forgot about how fat her arms were. "Will we move? Will you stay home?"

Harold started to laugh. "Well, to tell you the truth, your suggestions are both interesting and frightening to a man who doesn't know how to stop working as hard as he can. I'll have to cross that bridge when I come to it."

"No kidding, Daddy. Why don't we buy a camper and live on the road for a couple of years?" she teased.

The word *camper* immediately made Harold think of his older daughter, Suzanna, who had left for a California cooperative farm in a brightly painted camper. That move had been a devastatingly flagrant rejection of his lifestyle and values and everything he had wanted for Suzanna. Was his younger daughter now mocking him with her suggestion that he follow a path he had scorned so deeply only a few years before?

"A camper's a ridiculous idea! Do I look like some hippie relic from the sixties?" He overreacted so instinctively that he didn't realize she was only kidding.

Kessa's teasing mood vanished immediately. "No, you *don't* look like a hippie. But for a minute I thought you could be fun."

"Guys my age don't run around in campers. And besides, who's giving you two years off to roam around the country? You sound more like your sister every day."

Always Suzanna. "It just so happens that most camper owners are guys your age. You're no fun and you don't have any imagination."

Hal could think of nothing to say in self-defense. "Grace, why do they all start to sound the same—the kids, I mean."

"Maybe they have a point. A camper doesn't sound like such a bad idea, if you do ever retire. I wouldn't mind it one bit."

"What's for dessert?" He abruptly changed the subject.

Kessa stared at her plate and thought that if her father retired and spent all day with the family, he wouldn't have any secrets anymore. He'd probably go nuts, so it would never happen. Her mother would never be able to fully share his life. A bad deal for Mom. But then, she realized, her mom had had a bad deal from day one.

Grace wiped her lips anxiously, hoping that the argument wouldn't prevent her daughter from eating.

Harold wanted to leave the table as soon as possible to turn on the TV and forget about the future. As well as the present.

Why can't we communicate without everyone misinterpreting everything? Kessa wondered as she cleared the table. Does this happen in other families too? An image flashed in her mind of a blackboard, a seating arrangement: The second family therapy session during her hospitalization.

The first family therapy session had left all the Dietrichs feeling like failures. They'd spent most of the time arguing about Suzanna. As usual. Kessa had isolated herself in a corner, looking nearly catatonic.

This time Dr. Sherman staged the seating himself, making a chart on a hospital blackboard.

> Kessa   Suzanna
>
>   Sherman
>
> Harold   Grace

"Today," Sherman began, sounding like an autocratic maître d', "I will ask the family how each of you has been affected by Kessa's anorexia. I'm sure that it has mystified you, upset you, worried you, and caused you to rethink who this member of your family has turned into. And let me just say here how sorry I am that Gregg said he was too busy to come."

I'm not sorry at all, Kessa thought. *He'd never really do anything for me. And I wouldn't know what to say to him if he did come.*

"Okay. Let's begin with Suzanna," Sandy continued.

"First of all, who is Kessa?" she asked a bit sarcastically. "Is that Francesca's new nickname?"

Kessa stared at her sister.

"Kessa, I believe you have to answer that question," Sherman prompted.

Wanting to defy her family but not able to ignore Sandy's request, she hesitantly replied, "One day I decided that I didn't like Francesca anymore, so I shortened it to Kessa."

"Is that supposed to mean something significant?" Harold asked, turning toward Sherman.

"Probably."

Harold was annoyed. That wasn't an answer.

Sherman prompted again. "Suzanna, we were beginning with you, and though I can see that the family has difficulty focusing on this question, I'll ask it again. How has your sister's illness affected your feelings toward her?"

"Well, to be honest, I haven't seen Fr—Kessa, weird name—since all of this started. I've only seen her since she's been in the hospital. When I first saw her three weeks ago, I was shocked. I thought she was dying of cancer or something. There's something . . . yeah—colder, almost meaner about her. Sort of creepy. I don't know who she is anymore. And I guess I'm mad at her for putting my parents through all this."

"Suzanna, *you've* put us through all sorts of things for years, and we can tolerate this from your sister," Harold interjected. "Maybe it's just her turn."

"Yeah, well you sure sound reasonable here," Suzanna said, looking betrayed. "That's not what you say at home!"

"Suzanna, you find Kessa's behavior intimidating then?" Sherman intervened.

"Well, not exactly . . . it's just—" She looked across at her emaciated sister, the expressionless girl who had somehow replaced the lovable clown Francesca had once been. Her voice dropped to a choked whisper. "Whoever my sister has become is pretty intimidating . . . and saddening. Part of me wants to run away from her. Part of me wants to shake her as hard as I can until she snaps out of it."

"Mrs. Dietrich." Sherman's voice remained calmly authoritative. "Could you tell us how this has affected you?"

Tears were already forming in Grace's eyes, and she

reached for a tissue from the box Sandy had placed on the coffee table that served as a makeshift barricade. Kessa turned her head sharply away. Grace noticed, and her tears flowed more freely. "I think, Dr. Sherman, that you're already seeing how this has affected me."

Sherman waited for her to continue.

Harold wanted to rescue his wife. She'd gone through enough already. He reached for her hand, but she waved it off.

"My daughter's illness makes me feel like a complete failure and, like most people, I don't like to look at my failures. Except this isn't one I'm able to run away from, so I have to stay with it and that makes my angry. Sometimes I think that all my daughter's behavior is specifically designed to hurt or punish me, for God knows what."

"Mr. Dietrich, could you tell us how this has affected you?"

"What you see here is how this has affected me," he nearly shouted. "I'm troubled seeing what's happening to my wife. I don't know why my daughter needs to fight the whole world for the goal of starving herself, maybe to death. I'm angry and I'm confused."

"Dr. Sherman, does my sister know what she looks like?" Suzanna asked.

"Do you mean, is she crazy?" Sherman said.

"I didn't say that," Suzanna protested.

"Oh, I think you did and that's all right."

Sandy looked around at each of them. Their eyes all seemed to be out of focus. Each had retreated from this terrifying arena, unable to face it any longer. Kessa felt the silence most of all.

Sherman let them stew for a moment, then broke the silence. "Surely Kessa must seem somewhat crazy to you."

Silence. The fact that no one answered acknowledged his point.

"If you view Kessa as crazy, your expectations become lessened," he explained. "Perhaps your patience becomes greater. If Kessa had no legs, you wouldn't expect her to run races. Temporarily, Kessa has no ability to eat normally—even if her life depended upon it." He turned toward his patient. "Could you, Kessa?"

They all waited anxiously for her answer, hoping she would protest the accusation of "crazy."

"No. I guess not. Not yet anyway."

"So I guess we could say you're a bit crazy, for the present."

"I guess we could," she mumbled. She didn't feel insulted or even defeated, just glad it was out in the open,.

"My daughter isn't *crazy*," Harold protested. "She has a problem, that's all."

"Mr. Dietrich, how would you treat your daughter differently if you thought she were crazy?"

"I couldn't expect much from her. I'd feel hopeless about her."

"That's not quite what I asked," Sandy said gently. "That tells us how you'd *feel* about her, but I want to know how you would treat her, how you would deal with her if you thought she was crazy."

Maybe she really was crazy after all, Harold Dietrich thought. His eyes became wet. "I guess I would be less angry and more patient . . . but I don't *want* to deal with her as if she were crazy. . . . Won't that just keep her . . . crazy?"

"No, but it might just keep her safe." Sherman's reply was as soft as the question.

"Safe from what, Dr. Sherman?" Grace asked.

"Safe from your anger, your disappointment, your feelings of rejecting her."

"But we've always been proud of her," Grace protested.

"But not now."

"Now she's ... not well."

"Can you forgive her for being 'not well,' as you put it?"

"Well, of course. But how will that help?"

"It would help if I didn't have to feel inferior every time I see you," Kessa said. "It was bad enough when I walked by strangers and I heard them whispering about me. 'Look at her—she's got anorexia.' They'd say it loud enough so I could hear it. But when you visit me here and you look at me with that pained expression on your face, it's pretty obvious that you can't stand to look at me. It's like you won't like me anymore until I become someone else. Can't you still like me even though I'm like this?"

Grace got up and walked around her husband's chair to where her daughter was sitting. She hesitated, then leaned over to hug Kessa. "I can *love* you even though you're like this, honey," she said, involuntary tears staining her cheeks.

Kessa sat rigidly, not responding to her mother's embrace, but her eyes welled up too.

"So how do we treat her?" Harold asked, looking pointedly at Sherman and not at his wife.

"When she is crazy or incompetent, treat her like a crazy person. Be in charge of her, protective of her, and caring of her. When she's not crazy, treat her normally."

"But that's like having two people to deal with," Harold protested.

Sherman nodded. "It's complicated ... like being self-consciously loving."

"Then when can we relax?" Suzanna objected.

"When you're not with your sister."

"Dr. Sherman," Grace stated. "It sounds as if you're telling us not to be natural with Fran—Kessa."

"If you want your daughter to change in a profound way—to change from only trusting herself and her own behaviors to trusting others, you, her family—you will have to bring a new energy to your relation with Kessa. If she has to overcome this all by herself, it will take longer, and she may never be close to you."

"So it seems we all have problems to overcome." Harold attempted a weak smile.

Chapter
17

The mirror reflection stared back at her as Kessa stood contemplating her body, comparing it—for the first time ever, she realized—with her mother's. Grace had narrow shoulders, broad hips, and short legs. Kessa was broad at the shoulders, proportionately narrower at the hips, and her legs were much longer. She wondered if she would wake up one morning and find that overnight her body had metamorphosed into her mother's frame. Kessa knew she was being paranoid, but escape from this fate was imperative.

Looking at her body was too depressing. Kessa walked over to what she now called "the weight corner" of her room. There stood her brand new medical scale. She liked how it looked with its long, white spine and the collarbone-like structure that supported the balance bar with the sliding weights. She slid up the measuring rod and stood as tall as she could.

"Still five-four?" She talked to the scale as if it were a person, like she had talked to the mechanical pump that had force-fed her in the hospital. "If you said that I got taller I wouldn't care as much if I gained any weight."

She pushed the weights violently to the right. "Three hundred and fifty . . . fatso!"

She moved the larger weight back to the fifty notch and the smaller to forty-five. The bar tilted upward.

"Damn! Way into the nineties! Nearly over a hundred."

She pulled off her turtleneck and removed her shoes, jeans, socks, watch, earrings, the gold chain around her neck, and finally her rings. She allowed four ounces for her underwear and moved the lower weight once again.

"Ninety-eight at night! That's practically ninety-five in the morning!"

She dressed quickly in case her parents might knock. She thought briefly about taking a diuretic but remembered Dr. Gordon's lecture about diuretics, that they cause only temporary dehydration; they don't reduce the amount of body tissue, and real body weight is regained with every glass of liquid you drink. Then she wondered about laxatives, but remembered the cramps and diarrhea that always followed. Vomiting was out of the question. Seeing Deirdre vomit had permanently settled that issue.

Kessa returned to the mirror and saw a heavier girl than she had just observed minutes before. This girl in the mirror was fat. The scale had said so, condemning her at ninety-eight. She knew that her period would return at ninety-nine. Two pounds had to go. Right away. Just to be sure. Nobody would notice, and she would be safe.

"Why not bring your weight up to a menstrual weight?" Dr. Sherman was puzzled. She looked nearly normal, yet . . .

Kessa shrugged.

He pressed on. "Is it the inconvenience of the whole business?"

"It has nothing to do with the physical part. I don't mind that."

Sandy was stumped. "What does it signify to you, Kessa?"

"It's the last proof."

"Of what?"

"That I'm not completely normal," Kessa said quickly.

"Normal as opposed to what?"

Silence. Then: "You know, the way I was."

"You mean, it's coming from the part of you that's jealous of Deirdre?"

"Don't you think I weigh enough now?" Kessa seemed distressed.

"If you're frightened to gain more weight right now, don't"

"Then you *do* think that I weigh enough! You just don't want to tell me!"

"I think you've got me cornered and that makes you feel more powerful."

"You just won't tell me! I'm probably too fat already!"

"I don't believe that you mean what you just said," Sherman said quietly. "I believe that you're scared and you're confusing scared with fat."

Kessa bit her lip. Sandy was right, and she could never be angry with him when she knew he was right. Damn it all!

"Have I frightened you out of being angry?"

"No. It just went away," she admitted. "It's weird."

"So, if I make *fat* an illegal word here, you can't get angry?"

"It feels that way."

"Then we'll have to find you other, more appropriate

words that will let you get angry and stay angry for legitimate reasons."

"But how can you do that?"

"If I said, 'I want you to weigh enough to menstruate by next month,' what would you answer?"

She shrugged again.

"You could tell me that you'll do that when you're good and ready and not a moment before," Sandy offered.

"That would be hard for me to say."

"Isn't that the truth?"

"I guess so."

"So say it," Sherman challenged.

"I can't."

"Pretend it's an audition for a part in a play."

"I don't want my period"—her voice became strident—"and I may *never* want it!"

"That was terrific!"

"But I was faking," she protested.

"Faking will do for a start."

"But ... I don't like being angry at anyone. Why do people have to get angry?"

"You just got angry at me because you thought I'd make you fat and not tell you."

"That was different."

"You know what you're saying, Kessa? You're admitting that's the only issue you allow yourself to get angry about."

"I guess so."

"Then I can see why it's important for you not to be 'normal.' "

"I don't understand what you're saying."

Sandy searched for the right words. "Arguing to control your weight is the only time you permit yourself to confront someone else. If you lose your need to struggle over keeping your weight down, you lose your ability to struggle over anything. Then all you can be is a nice kid who doesn't ever stick up for herself."

"That's a horrible idea." She glared at the floor.

"If you think that it's such a horrible idea, then between now and our next meeting try to confront someone who's not a member of your family but who says something or does something that hurts you—hurts your feelings or makes you feel taken advantage of."

"Why shouldn't it be someone in my family?"

"Because your family's so frightened of your losing weight that you have an unfair advantage," Sandy said bluntly.

"That makes me sound awful to my family," Kessa complained.

"Not half as awful as you are to yourself. If someone else had done to you all the things that you've done to yourself in the past year, they'd be lynched."

"Why do I do it? . . . I mean, why *did* I do it?" Kessa was genuinely bewildered. For a minute she was able to look back at herself as if she were observing a total stranger.

"I guess it was the only way you could feel safe—and powerful."

"Will I ever stop? Sometimes I think that I'll always be stuck like this."

"Have things changed for you in the last year?"

"Yes," Kessa replied firmly.

"Then we'll just have to make sure that they can keep changing at the same rate until you're satisfied!"

"You don't understand. I'll never be satisfied!"

"Then we'll never be finished . . . will we?" Sandy smiled.

"Does it count if I confront *you*?"

"You get part credit."

As Kessa walked down the street to catch the bus, her

head was a jumble of ideas: Was Sherman calling her selfish? Didn't he understand how scared she still was? Would she hate her body for the rest of her life? She was starting to get a headache.

The more she replayed the afternoon's session, the more Kessa became angry at Dr. Sherman. She wanted to tell him that he really didn't have all the answers, that he had never suffered from anorexia and couldn't really understand how it felt. He'd *never* understand that.

Kessa slowly passed a few coffee shops, and she looked at the women inside. The men didn't matter—it was as if they were a species apart, immune to women's problems about eating and weight control. Kessa saw two slender, elegantly dressed women picking at the food on the plates in front of them. Salads, with dressing on the side; tuna with lemon wedges; no rolls.

Kessa hurried up the block to another restaurant and peered in the window. Sure enough, there were more women toying with their canteloupes and cottage cheese or ignoring poached eggs on dry toast.

He's lying to me! She almost said it out loud. All these women always on diets, and he's telling me I don't have to worry about gaining weight! Some of them are thinner than me and they're just pretending to eat stupid salads. And I'm supposed to sit around and get fatter while the whole dieting world passes me by. Then I'll really be the loser. *The thinner is the winner.* Deirdre was right, after all. Sandy doesn't know what he's doing. I can't trust him to make important decisions about my weight for me. I can't trust anybody but *myself.*

Chapter
18

For the next week Kessa modified her food intake. Breakfast was bran flakes with skim milk, lunch was a cucumber, and dinner a one-egg "puffy" omelette—egg white whipped separately—with lettuce and tomato. Carbohydrates—bread, potatoes, and rice—were barely touched.

Sherman noticed immediately that she looked thinner.

"Kessa, your hospital discharge weight was one hundred and one pounds. I think we should weigh you to see what's happening."

"I'll tell you what's happening. I'm getting fat as a pig!"

"If you are, it will show up on the scale."

She walked over to his scale, forced each shoe off at the heel with the toe of the other, and mounted it as if she were Joan of Arc about to be tied to the stake. She stood there, waiting for him to move the weights. He set them at one hundred. The bar dropped. She was elated.

"Ninety-five, nope. Ninety-four . . . nope." His voice was becoming flat, concealing any signs of disappointment or anger.

She watched the scale, poker-faced, while he adjusted the weights.

"Ninety-one." The bar finally balanced.

They both remained expressionless as she dismounted, put her shoes on, and resumed her seat on the couch.

Kessa peered at him through her eyelashes. He was trying very hard not to show how he felt, but the stiffness in his voice was a dead giveaway.

"I guess it was too close to menstruation for comfort."

"It had nothing to do with that," she lied. "I was just getting too fat."

"You were getting too scared."

"That's your *interpretation*, Doctor," Kessa said, trying to hide her rage under glib sarcasm.

"Kessa, you're *not* getting too fat. It's far more complicated than that."

"You just like fat girls, that's all. I believe you when you say you don't think I was getting fat, but I'm not so sure you would really know if I was or not."

"You said the same thing to me at seventy pounds, you know. You would have said the same thing to me at fifty pounds, except you wouldn't have been alive to say it. No weight has ever felt low enough to you."

Kessa opened her mouth to protest. *The thinner is the winner*. But what would she have won? She stared at the floor, the familiar "blanking-out" look on her face. Sandy watched all her conflicting emotions dance across her features. They were both thinking about how much she had weighed in the hospital.

It had been a rough day and Sandy Sherman was thinking that he wanted nothing more than to hurry home and soak some of his tension away in his bathtub when the phone rang. He was sorely tempted to let his machine pick up the call. He stared at the ringing phone for several seconds, then realized the machine wasn't turned on. Reluctantly, he reached over the desk and answered.

"Hi. It's me. Kessa."

"What is it, Kessa?"

"Is this the wrong time to call?"

"I'm on my way out, but since you reached me, what's up?"

"I just wanted to know when I'm leaving the hospital. I've been here five weeks. It's been nearly three weeks since family therapy started, and I weigh eighty-nine pounds. I'm eating everything that I'm supposed to, so when can I leave?"

"Kessa, I don't want to give you a date off the top of my head since I would invariably change it after thinking about it. We have a goal weight of a hundred and one pounds before you leave the hospital."

"But can't I gain the rest of it at home?" she protested. "You're the one who's always talking about trust. Is that only for me to trust you, or are you ever going to trust me as well?"

"Kessa, I don't want to get into this right now. I'll talk to you about it when I get to the hospital tomorrow morning."

"Oh great. Go home and rehearse your lines so you know what bullshit to say to me tomorrow. Good bye!" She slammed down the phone.

Sandy stared at the phone the way Kessa often stared at the floor. Then he put on the answering machine and headed for home.

He walked into her room the next morning to find her pouting and refusing to make eye contact.

"Good morning, Kessa." He forced himself to be cheer-ful. "We can use the small conference room instead of the classroom today. It's a more appropriate size for two people to talk in, anyway." His voice trailed off a little as he realized she wouldn't answer him.

In silence, Kessa slowly got out of bed, dragging the IV with her.

She wants to punish me for not letting her go home at eighty-nine pounds, Sandy thought as they walked into the conference room. If she succeeds in forcing me to give in or making me mad at her, I've failed her. Then she'll be angry at me for more important reasons.

"Kessa," he said aloud, "The expression on your face looks like a continuation of yesterday's phone conversation."

"I told you that I wanted to go home and gain the rest of my weight there," she said coldly.

"You also told me something about it being a matter of trust."

She nodded.

"I don't agree. I think it's more a matter of responsibility—my responsibility to you to be in charge of treatment. In this case it means to determine, in consultation with Dr. Donaldson, the length of your hospitalization. I have discussed it with him and you've got a few more pounds to gain. That looks like a few weeks more."

That was it. She was stuck here till she got as fat as an elephant. Kessa went over every plea she could think of in her head, then ventured, "I know that I don't really want to gain more weight than this, even though I'm supposed to.

"I also know that this appearance seems very thin to you, but it's the most I've weighed in a long time. If this makes me fat, I'll never forgive you."

"I want to help you make weight and appearance something you don't have to drown in for the rest of your life," Sandy said. "None of us wants to make you fat. If I let you get fat, you would drown in that too. There's too much to do in life than spending it obsessed with the weight and shape of your body."

It was all just words. Kessa regarded her arms and legs. She was going to get fat and nothing he could say would convince her it wasn't true.

Kessa didn't want to think about the hospital anymore. She focused her thoughts on the present. "No weight has ever felt low enough to you," Sandy had said. *That's not fair!* she wanted to protest.

Then she looked up at him as if she were about to deliver the *coup de grace.* "You're just trying to make me look crazy."

Sandy ignored her comment and changed his tack. "How badly do you want to win this argument?"

"What do you mean?"

"Well, it appears that we're not trying to resolve our differences but trying to defeat each other. You're casting me in the villain's role in order to win, but I don't want to defeat you. As a matter of fact, I don't want you defeated by anyone."

"I just don't want to be pushed around, that's all."

"I'm glad you're arguing. Now, the next step is to argue for something more worthwhile than whether you're fat or not. You've been able to argue about that since before you went to the hospital."

"Well, I just don't know when I have a right to argue," Kessa said. She was starting to feel a little helpless.

"You felt that you had a right to argue with me just now."

"But that's what you just told me. The only thing I can argue about is my weight or my appearance."

"Didn't you argue with Deirdre about her vomiting?"

"Hey, that's right!" Kessa felt a little better. "But I don't know if I'll ever feel comfortable arguing like most people do."

"We'll just have to monitor it the way we do your weight. I suspect that as you learn not to transfer all your anger to ideas about being fat, you'll discover you can use it to protect yourself from being dominated by other people's words and wishes."

"Well that sure sounds good, but I still don't know how it's going to happen." Now she was skeptical, but at least that was a whole lot better than being scared and helpless.

"Tell you what," Sandy said. "Work on confronting someone who offends you this week. See what terrible thing happens to you."

"Very funny, Dr. Sherman," Kessa said. "I think you're going to get me into trouble."

"Maybe you should find out what happens if you do get into a little trouble."

Kessa took his advice literally. She decided to go to Skirmishes that Friday night.

"Hello, Deirdre."

"Kessa?"

"Yeah, listen. Do you want to go to Skirmishes tomorrow night with me?"

"What's Skirmishes?" She sounded really tired. Her voice was hardly more than a whisper.

"Now you sound like me." Kessa liked the feeling of being the more sophisticated one for a change. "Skirmishes is a bar that serves high school kids like us."

"What are we going to do in a bar?"

"Look at guys. Maybe get picked up or something."

"I'd rather stay home."

"Don't be such a baby. You do go out with guys, don't you?"

"Well ... not lately," Deirdre sounded completely intimidated.

"Look, I'm really not so experienced myself." Kessa wondered if Deirdre was as uninterested and as inexperienced with boys as she was. "But I think it will do both of us a lot of good."

"All right, although it sounds pretty boring to me."

Pretty terrifying was more like it.

Chapter
19

Skirmishes seemed just the same to Kessa, except maybe it wasn't quite as sinister because now she knew her way around. She led Deirdre to a small table near the bar, then sat down and stared at the guys, the way the girls from school did.

Most of the men seemed to be in their late twenties or older, although there were a few boys around her age. It was hard to tell in the dark room.

"I don't think we should've come here, Kessa."

"Why not?"

"It gives me the creeps. All the guys here are older than us." Deirdre sat hunched over the table. She was too nervous to take her jacket off.

"What would we want with guys our age, anyway?"

"I never knew you were so experienced, Kessa."

"I'm not. But I'm going to be, damnit."

"Oh great! I'm sitting in this disgusting place just to take part in your experiment to see if you can get some experience."

"Well, don't you like guys?"

"I don't know."

Deirdre's vulnerability made Kessa feel a little nervous. It reminded her of how she was bluffing. Well, this evening was her idea, and she was determined to stick it out. "What's the big deal?" she asked.

"You're so full of it. I think you're faking this whole thing to prove something to yourself."

"You're right, you know. We've got a lot of stuff to prove to ourselves and this is as good a time as any to prove it."

"Oh, right," Deirdre said with absolutely no conviction, "It's a change from staring at the toilet, anyway."

"Hey, see those two guys over there?"

Deirdre peered over at the bar. "You mean the checked shirt and the work shirt?"

"Yeah. Don't you think they're kind of cute?"

They were, actually, but Deirdre wasn't about to admit it. "I think they look like assholes. They're probably just out for something we can't produce.

"Like what?"

"Like getting laid."

Deirdre's bluntness startled Kessa, and it made her eye the guys with a little more trepidation. One was blond and one was dark. They were both tall and thin, and held cigarettes loosely. More like props than an addiction. They both seemed pretty tired, too; their eyes were nearly closed from fatigue. Since they looked too tired for trouble, Kessa decided it was okay to look in their direction. They caught her gaze and smiled at each other, saying something while pointing toward Kessa and Deirdre. Then they straightened up, grabbed their beers, and walked toward them.

"Kessa, those guys are coming over." If a whisper could sound hysterical, Deirdre's did.

"Couldn't we be cool about it? I mean, so what's the big deal?"

Kessa was actually as frightened as Deirdre, but she was still determined to fake it.

"Can we sit down?"

That didn't sound so awful. Kessa felt a little bit more confident. "Sure," she said, not quite trusting her voice as she pointed to two unoccupied chairs near their table.

"Do you come here often?" the dark-haired one asked Kessa. He didn't look at her directly. Maybe he was shy, too. Or maybe he was astute enough to pick up on Kessa's shyness.

Kessa looked at her friend. It almost seemed like Deirdre was her conscience or something.

"I—we've been here a couple of times."

"My name's Tony, and this is Hugh. We're in construction."

"Yeah," Hugh snorted. "I'm into building."

Kessa wondered why Hugh was being cryptic. Maybe he wasn't in construction and he was really a dealer or something. She remembered her schoolmates' comments about the drug deals done at Skirmishes. She knew lots of kids at school who bought and sold grass, hash, and cocaine. Sometimes she thought everyone did it but her. And Deirdre, of course.

Kessa gave Deirdre a quick smile for reassurance, but her friend was looking at the door as if she would make a dash for it any moment. Then she took a sip of her club soda.

"So where do you work?" she asked.

"Oh, all over," Tony said. He still hadn't looked her in the eye. "Depends on the contractor."

Kessa tried to keep him talking—it was easier to listen than to have to think of something interesting to say about herself. "Do you make a lot of money?"

"Sometimes. You can make a lot workin' overtime."

"Can someone point me to the ladies' room?" Deirdre interrupted.

Oh God, she's going to throw up, Kessa thought in a panic. But she wasn't about to go baby-sit her friend. She'd tough it out and, surprisingly, she sort of liked playing the role of admiring female listening to the guy talk. She wanted to know his secrets, what he really did at work. What he liked.

Deirdre stood up.

"If you go back to the hallway leading to the front door, it's to the left of the telephone booth," Kessa explained.

Deirdre tried to smile as she hurried from the table.

Hugh seemed relieved. She wasn't his type. He murmured a "See-ya" to Tony and disappeared into the back room.

Kessa hoped Deirdre would get back soon. Her eyes followed the skinny girl as she dodged waitresses and customers. No one paid her any attention at all. Kessa played with her straw, then glanced at other tables to see what was happening. There were some other couples her age, and she watched the nodding and the smiling, the guys seeming to do most of the talking and the girls seeming to do most of the obligatory admiring. *A stranger looking at me would think I fit right in*, Kessa thought in amazement. She actually felt a little proud of her ability to fake this scene, one so alien and terrifying to her.

Fifteen minutes passed, and Deirdre had not returned.

"Why don't we leave?" Tony said quickly.

The question startled her. That meant game time was over.

"I have to find my friend. Maybe she's not feeling good."

"Will you be back?"

"Okay. Give me a few minutes."

Kessa hurried down the dark hallway. The ladies' room was empty. She did a quick walk through the bar. No Deirdre. She must have slipped out when Kessa wasn't looking. What should I do? Kessa wondered. She's probably not home yet, so I'll call her later.

Tony was waiting for her at the front door. "I paid the check," he said. "I've been waiting for you."

"Oh! Well thanks, but I can get home by myself."

"Who said anything about getting home?" he said teasingly. He wasn't quite so shy anymore. It's early. I live two blocks away. Do you want to come over?"

"Oh, I don't know."

"Your friend left, didn't she?"

"Yeah, she wasn't feeling well tonight."

"You look like you're feeling well tonight," he said, still teasing.

"Sure. Let's go." Kessa could not believe these words were coming out of her mouth.

They walked for a few blocks in silence. Kessa was glad he didn't try to take her hand or anything. If he touched her, she'd probably run screaming down the street.

It was cold out. Kessa felt a chill run through her and realized they'd been walking for quite a while. "Hey, I thought you lived two blocks away. We've already walked about nine."

"I'm sorry," Tony said contritely. "I forgot which bar we were at."

Was he telling the truth or trying to put the moves on? Kessa couldn't tell. "So where *do* you live?"

"Right here—the one with the two white globes."

She glanced up at the nondescript facade. It resembled all the other buildings on the street, but to a girl who had grown up in a luxurious high-rise with a doorman, it looked almost ominous. She took a step back and scanned the windows. Many had no curtains. It seemed deserted.

"C'mon up. Don't let the lobby scare you. It's a safe building, and I've got a nice apartment." His voice came out squeaky. He must be nervous too.

They walked into the lobby. The cracked and scuffed tiles almost made it look like a bathroom. Kessa stole a glance at Tony. His dark, straight hair and deep-set brown eyes made him look strong-willed, but his anxious smile betrayed an eager boyishness. He was handsome but still more of a boy than a man. If he had acted any more mature or threatening, Kessa could never have decided to prove to herself that she could be alone with a guy and not freak out for good.

They got off the elevator on the fourth floor. The roughness of the stuccolike plaster walls was accentuated by the bare hanging light bulbs in the hallway. It was a long way to Central Park West.

"Four D—that's me." Tony pointed.

She waited while he opened the three locks in his steel door. "Looks like a bank vault, Tony," she joked.

"Are you from out of town?"

"If you call Central Park West out of town, then I am."

"Well, I don't know what you're so surprised about. Everyone I know has three or even more locks on their doors."

At last the door swung open, and Kessa caught her breath in surprise. Tony had a nice place—thick moss-green wall-to-wall carpeting, black lacquered shelving, and a comfortable black leather sofa and chairs. The living room was dominated by a huge color television, VCR, and stereo system, and records were piled everywhere. He had a grown-up's apartment. She thought of her parents' antique furniture and how different Tony's place was. He must really be doing well in the construction business.

He watched her take it all in. "Hey, you wanna hear some music? I just got a new tape deck." He waved at the stacks of records. "I've been making tapes. Sorry for the mess."

"It's okay," she said nervously.

"Do you like Bruce Springsteen?" .

"Who doesn't?"

Tony put a record on and disappeared into the kitchen. Kessa wiped her palms on her jeans and sat on one of the overstuffed chairs. That way he wouldn't be able to sit next to her and try anything funny.

Tony came in with an opened bottle of white wine and a plate of cheese and crackers. He poured the wine as if his greatest concern was not spilling any on his coffee table. Kessa found his manner reassuring, so she decided to try a glass of wine.

"Would you like some cheese?" he asked.

"No thanks."

He raised his glass. "Here's to meeting at Skirmishes."

Kessa stared at the wine suspiciously for an instant and then drank with him.

"Would you like to see a movie?"

"Sure. You pick it."

He put on *Casablanca* and dimmed the lights. After half an hour, the wine bottle was empty. Kessa realized it was the fourth time she'd seen that movie.

Tony surreptitiously studied her face as she watched, taking in the still sharp jawline, the small nose dominated by large eyes and a full mouth. Her blunt-cut hair was falling in her face as she began to slump a little in her chair. He wondered if she streaked her hair, since it was not quite blond. He decided she probably didn't. She didn't look like the kind of girl who would bleach her hair. He thought she was pretty, and innocent and vulnerable—everything he liked in a girl.

He got up from the couch and sat down on the arm of her chair.

"How's the movie?"

"Fine, thanks. I've seen it before." Kessa's voice was a bit woozy. She shouldn't have had anything to drink.

Tony gently reached over and brushed Kessa's hair back off her face. Then he slid over so that he was nearly sitting on top of her on the chair. Kessa instinctively moved over before she realized what he was doing.

He put his arms around her and pulled her close so that her breasts were now pressed up against his chest. Kessa's heart began to thump wildly, and she felt the heat of terror spreading through her veins. She remained motionless, her limbs frozen in panic. He bent to kiss her.

"What do you think you're doing?" she yelled, arching her back so violently that she nearly fell off the chair.

Startled by her reaction, Tony stood up. Where was this girl coming from? He'd been pretty cool—and he certainly hadn't forced himself on her.

"Hey," he said, trying to calm her down. "I just wanted to give you a hug. Be affectionate, you know. I'm sorry it got you upset."

"Bullshit! Be affectionate somewhere else! What are these things?" she shouted, pointing to her breasts. "Magnets? And what's it supposed to do for me?"

"I said I was sorry. I really like you, Kessa. I'd never try to do anything if I thought it would make you angry. I thought you liked me, too."

"What does liking me have to do with grabbing me?" Kessa's heart was still thumping, and all the wine and her adrenaline made her far more assertive than she'd ever dreamed she could be.

"Don't you like that?" an incredulous Tony asked. This

girl was out to lunch. Everyone liked to make out.

"I think it's stupid to have some guy poking and squeezing me, and I wonder what the hell he's getting out of it while I'm just getting sore and probably black and blue."

"I thought that was a turn-on for you, and romantic and everything."

"Wrong, and wrong! It just makes me wish I didn't have these things you like to grab so much. Maybe you could find some other way to be romantic."

"I said I'm sorry." What did she want from him?

Kessa pulled on her coat. "Are you going to be a gentleman and get me a cab?"

She leaned on the elevator button as Tony triple-locked his door. He decided she was crazy, but he still liked her. She decided there was nothing she wanted more than to be safe in her own bed.

Luckily, a cab came by right away. Kessa leaped in and slammed the door.

Tony rapped on the window. "Could I see you again?" he mouthed.

She turned her face away as the cab drove off into the night.

Chapter
20

Kessa stayed awake all night, staring at the ceiling. She remembered when she had first started to diet, how she'd stand for hours in front of the full-length mirror in her parents' room, enraged at her developing body, wishing her breasts would go away and disappear. At seventy-two pounds they had, along with all the rest of the fat tissue on her body. She used to lie awake for hours then too, feeling her body . . .

Now for the test of how lean. Kessa ran her fingers over her stomach. Flat. But was it flat enough? Not quite. She still had some way to go. *Just to be safe,* she told herself. Still, it was nice the way her pelvic bones rose like sharp hills on either side of her stomach. Kessa picked up her head and looked down at her breasts. Flatter, but still not flat enough . . .

But now that body was becoming normal, and what made her a woman was already getting her into trouble. Guys would start expecting—demanding—things from her. And who had put her in this position? Dr. Sandy Sherman. He was the one who had forced her to gain all this weight. Sandy was the villain, and everything was his fault.

As the hours slowly ticked by, Kessa thought morning would never come. She looked at the slowly moving hands on her clock every ten minutes. By the time it was eight-thirty in the morning, she decided to call Sherman at home. It was Saturday, but he had kids, she reasoned, and would probably be awake.

"Hello?" He picked up the phone, his voice hoarse.

"Hi. This is Kessa."

"Who?"

"Kessa. I'm sorry to disturb you at home, but I needed to talk to you about something."

"I'm sorry, Kessa. I'm not awake yet. Could you call back at ten, or is it an emergency?"

"No. It's not an emergency. 'Bye." She hung up, enraged. Where was Sandy when she needed him? *I was nearly raped,* she thought, *and he was too sleepy to talk about it! I never should have trusted him to begin with!*

The angrier she became with Sherman, the less angry she became with Tony. He really did seem unhappy about her being mad at him, and he had wanted to see her again. She shouldn't have been so rude. He was a guy, after all, and she was just a girl. A dumb girl. A dumb *fat* girl. No, it wasn't Sandy's fault or Tony's fault. It was *hers*.

Kessa's anger shifted to its usual place—herself. Her body was the cause of all this trouble! It had made Tony pounce on her. As she lay back on her bed, gazing down the full length of her body, she wanted to punish the hated thing. She wanted to make it skinny again.

Kessa threw up breakfast and lunch. She thought about how awful it looked when she saw Deirdre do it, but her violent mood overrode her disgust.

After she finished getting rid of lunch, she walked out of the bathroom to find her mother waiting for her.

"Kessa, it's Saturday and you're just hanging around. Don't you have any plans?"

"I've got a hangover."

"A hangover?" Grace had to smile. When she saw Kessa bolt for the bathroom after lunch she'd felt pangs of anxiety, but an adolescent drinking spree was an almost welcome relief in comparison to Kessa's starvation, emaciation, near death in the hospital, and all the struggling they had been through.

"Yeah, I went out with a guy and drank too much."

"A boy from school?" Grace was starting to get concerned after all.

"No. Somebody I met at a bar."

"A bar?" Her mother's concern turned to alarm. "Why are you going to bars? You're not even eighteen. They're not supposed to let you in."

"Mom, there are bars around where they don't ask how old you are. Besides, most of the people there are kids from school anyway," she said, though that wasn't quite true about Skirmishes. "Oh, stop looking so worried."

Kessa walked into her room and slammed the door, then took off her robe and stood once more in front of the full-length mirror. Fat. She was getting fat. She picked up the phone and called Deirdre's house again. No answer. That was weird. Kessa frowned as she hung up. She knew Deirdre's parents were due back from one of their semimonthly jaunts to their condominium in Key Largo, Florida, that afternoon. Deirdre was usually very conscientious about cleaning the house before they returned. They commuted between their huge duplex apartment on Park Avenue and their marina home in Key Largo. New York was obligation; Florida, their new life.

Deirdre was a change-of-life baby, the youngest of three daughters in the McGuire family. Her sisters were twenty-eight and twenty-four, both married, and Deirdre was already an aunt. She often referred to herself as "the accident" and loved to quote her parents, who called her "the surprise." Deirdre felt guilty that she was preventing her parents from enjoying their "retirement years," as she put it, and shooed them off to Florida. Her parents went, ashamed yet grateful. They were too old to cope with an adolescent. But Deirdre gave them no arguments, no real cause for worry, even though she was a bit obsessive about dieting. Her father said it was just a phase—everyone wanted to be thin. Her mother wasn't so sure, but she couldn't bear to criticize her baby. After all, Deirdre was like the best little girl in the world to them.

Kessa dialed the McGuires' number again. Still no answer. She'd just have to keep trying.

Deirdre had slipped out of Skirmishes, conscientiously stopping in the ladies' room as she said she would. She quickly walked home, worried that something might happen to Kessa if she were left at Skirmishes alone, but far too frightened to stay with her.

She entered the apartment through the maid's door, which led directly into the long, narrow kitchen, then headed into the living room, where a wet bar had been built. It was a six-foot mahogany counter with a slate top, not unlike the bar at Skirmishes. Deirdre pulled out the bottle of vodka, poured herself half a twelve-ounce glass and added ice, tonic, and two lemon slices. Then she turned on the stereo, put one foot on the brass footrail, and gulped it all down.

It was an ironic contrast, the sticklike figure taking up half a bar stool in the McGuires' enormous living room,

where all the furniture was cushy and overstuffed and soft.
Deirdre was taking up less and less space in one of the
largest apartments in Manhattan.

She stayed at the bar for a while, tears silently streaming
down her cheeks as she pounded the slate countertop. She
almost expected a bartender to materialize to listen to her
problems.

Deirdre finished her drink, turned off the stereo, and
staggered into the kitchen. She looked at the clock on the
stove. Eleven-thirty. Time for a snack. She went to the
pantry and took out a box of chocolate chip cookies. At first
she ate them almost delicately, then she put a whole cookie
in her mouth at a time. Soon one cookie was crowded on top
of another and crumbs fell all over her mother's glossy tiled
floor as Deirdre ate what she could. When more than two
dozen cookies had been crammed in, Deirdre got up and
staggered to the little bathroom off the kitchen, lifted the
toilet seat, and threw up.

She wiped her face with a towel and returned to the
kitchen, opening the refrigerator door and taking out a
whole glazed ham. She sliced it and ate the slices with her
hands. Then she opened a can of pineapple and ate a few
slices with her hands as well. The ham and pineapple made
a combination of saltiness and sweetness that she liked to
mix. When she felt her stomach stretching to its limit, she
staggered back to the bathroom. She barely made it to the
toilet this time—leaning over and vomiting as if she were in
some bizarre relay race—then hurried back to the kitchen.
This time she ran her thumb through the holes of the
remaining pineapple slices and, grasping the end of the ham
with the other hand, ate as she walked to the bathroom. She
stood there over the toilet, alternately eating and vomiting,
unable to tell whether food was going down or coming up.

She went back to the kitchen for peanut butter, wrenched

the top of the jar off, and began to eat it with a tablespoon. Halfway through the jar, she could feel a numbness above her upper lip. Her thigh muscles were beginning to cramp and her fingertips tingled. She became worried about not being able to vomit up all of the high-calorie peanut butter, so she gulped down a twenty-four-ounce bottle of diet cola. But it made her feel worse. Perspiring and trembling, hardly able to coordinate her movements, she stumbled toward the bathroom, slapping her sticky hands against the cabinet doors and then the glossy tiled walls as she neared the bathroom. She saw the soda come up but only some of the peanut butter, so she went back for another bottle of cola. She drank it so fast she thought the gas in her stomach might explode inside of her. Her heart beat violently and her legs could barely support her. Her mouth involuntarily twisted as she again pressed curling, tightening fingers against the walls to guide herself back to the toilet. Dizzy and breathless, Deirdre was momentarily relieved when she saw the peanut butter come up. But something was very wrong with her body. It made her angry, then frightened. Her heartbeat now felt like a fist punching in her chest. All her limbs trembled and her mouth continued to twitch. She sat down in front of the toilet, unable to calm her convulsing body. As her hands gripped the wet seat, her eyes blurred and her hair stuck to the sides of her sweat-drenched face. The muscles around her mouth spasmed, pulling her lips to one side. The room darkened as she slipped from consciousness, and it didn't hurt when her head hit the floor.

When Clayton and Irene McGuire arrived home at four that Saturday afternoon, the first thing they noticed was that all the living room lights were on and an opened bottle of vodka stood next to the empty glass on the bar.

Clayton McGuire, a tall, graying man in his sixties, was

annoyed. "She just has too much freedom. We should have
sent her to boarding school," he grumbled to his wife.

Irene McGuire walked into the kitchen, where all the
lights were on as well. She was a handsome woman in her
late fifties, tanned and wiry, but when she surveyed the
kitchen, saw the mess, and smelled the vomit, deep lines of
worry etched her face. She followed the trail of sugar and
gravy handprints along the wall to the maid's bathroom.
There, lying on her side on the floor, to the left of a cola and
peanut butter-filled toilet, was her daughter. Her mouth was
open, and her left front tooth rested on the rim of the toilet.
Her skin was as pale as the glossy white tiles in the kitchen.

Irene touched her daughter's face. Cold as ice. As cold as
the numbing tentacles of fear that were spreading through
her body. She called Deirdre's name, softly at first, and then
her voice rose in hysteria as disbelief surrendered to horrify-
ing reality. She started to scream.

Clayton McGuire ran into the bathroom and saw his
daughter. He stood there uncomprehending. "What's
happened?"

"She's dead!"

"Why? From what?"

"She's dead . . . look at her! Touch her!" She slid to the
floor, cradled Deirdre's head in her lap, and began to sob.
The body was getting stiff.

Clayton was numb with shock. "My God, she's so thin."

"She's dead."

"When did she lose all that weight?" His voice sounded
disembodied.

"She's dead," his wife repeated dully.

"Oh God," he whispered. "We have to call the police."

"No!" she screamed. "They'll take her away! I don't want
them to take her away!"

Clayton pounded the wall with his fist. They'd have to take her away. She was gone forever.

Kessa kept dialing the McGuires' number. At first there was no answer, and then it was busy all the time. She was desperate to tell Deirdre about the previous night, desperate to tell her that Sherman had let her down, desperate to know that she'd gotten home safely. It was late in the afternoon before she got through.

Clayton answered the phone with a weak hello.

"This is Kessa Dietrich. May I please speak with Deirdre?"

"Are you a friend of hers?"

"Yes."

"I'm sorry." He started to sob. Kessa felt a chill run all the way down her spine. Something had happened. Something awful. "I'm so sorry . . ."

"Is this Mr. McGuire?" Her voice was starting to shake.

"Yes. I'm sorry, but when we arrived home, we found her dead in the bathroom."

Kessa sat paralyzed in shock. Tears involuntarily formed in her eyes. It couldn't be true.

"I'm sorry. I have to go now. Goodbye." He hung up.

Kessa sat holding the telephone, the dial tone buzzing in her ear. Deirdre couldn't be dead. It was impossible.

Moving like a robot, she cradled the receiver and lay down on her bed. Then she took a pillow and placed it over her mouth so her mother wouldn't hear her screams.

Chapter
21

Kessa walked into Sherman's waiting room and sat down. She looked at the other two girls sitting there and wondered if they would die too. They were both incredibly thin. Absorbed in their reading, they didn't notice Kessa's scrutiny. One was avidly scanning the food ads in a magazine; the other was reading a romance novel.

Sherman appeared at the door. "Kessa, come in." His greeting was annoyingly measured as usual.

He looked at her closely. Her eyes were puffy and her hands were trembling. "You look pale. Is anything the matter?"

Kessa stared at the floor, then automatically reached for a tissue to wipe her eyes. It took her a few minutes to gather the courage to tell Sandy what had happened. If she didn't say it, then it wasn't true.

But it was true.

"Deirdre's dead," she whispered.

Sandy was shocked. He wanted to press Kessa for all the

details, but he knew she'd have to volunteer any information.

"I called her house all day Saturday. Nobody answered
until late in the afternoon. Oh yeah, I called you early that
morning. Sorry if I disturbed you." She smiled sadly, mocking her need to call him at home. "I was mad at you that
morning because you couldn't talk to me and I needed to
talk about what happened to me the night before. I don't
even care about the night before anymore. While something
stupid was happening to me, something worse was happening to Deirdre . . . she was dying . . . I guess."

"Has anyone told you what happened to her?"

"I think she died at home. I don't know if she killed
herself or had an accident or what." She began to cry in
earnest. "I want to know what happened to her. She was my
friend. Maybe if I hadn't taken her to Skirmishes that night
she would still be all right. I feel like I killed her."

She blew her nose, but the tears wouldn't stop. "I have to
find out what happened to her," she said between sobs. "We
have the same doctor. Dr. Gordon. I'll ask her." She blew
her nose again, then leaned back on the couch and stuck her
fists in her eyes. "But no matter what, she'll still be dead. I
don't want her to be dead."

Sandy thought he'd never felt so helpless with a patient.
There was no way he could possibly ease her grief.

After a few minutes, Kessa calmed down a little.

"Do you want to talk about it?" Sandy asked very gently.

"Maybe I did kill her. Maybe it was my fault, because I
made her go to Skirmishes with me. What am I going to do
if it was my fault?" Kessa started to sob again.

"Kessa, listen to me," Sandy said sternly. "You cannot
blame yourself. Do you remember when you told me how
she literally wrestled you out of the way when she had to get
rid of that pizza? Do you remember how helpless you felt?"

Kessa nodded slowly.

"Kessa, Deirdre had bulimia. She had to throw up. There was nothing you could have done."

"Maybe there was. Why couldn't I have done something else?

Sandy had no answer.

"I'm grateful you don't have anything to say," Kessa said as she pulled on her coat. "I wouldn't believe it."

Kessa hurried out of Sherman's office. She had to know what had killed Deirdre.

Where was a newsstand? She stopped abruptly on the sidewalk, and the pedestrian behind her nearly knocked her down. But Kessa was oblivious—to all the pedestrians, to the windows filled with expensive merchandise, to the daily bustle of Madison Avenue. Then she remembered there was a newsstand a few blocks away, on Seventy-sixth Street. The papers would tell her.

The tiny shop had magazines overflowing the shelves and foreign as well as domestic newspapers were stacked to the ceiling. Kessa scanned the racks intently.

"Can I help you?" the man behind the counter asked.

"Oh, I'd like all of today's papers."

"Young lady, I got sixty-five different papers here. You can't read Greek, Italian, and Russian, can you?"

"No. The New York papers, I mean. The *Times*, the *News*, and the *Post*."

"It's your lucky day," he joked. "For you, I got all three." He handed her the newspapers as she rummaged in her purse for change. "You doin' a current events project for school or somethin'?"

"No, not for school. For myself." She paid for the papers and walked back out into the dull sunshine, heading west for Central Park until she found an unoccupied bench.

She sat down and, beginning with the *Times*, began to turn pages. She checked the headlines for "Suicide," "Teenager," "Deirdre...," "Upper East Side," "Teen Death," even the obituaries. But no luck. Half an hour later she stared down at her frozen ink-smudged hands, totally discouraged and depressed. There was no mention of Deirdre's death anywhere. She would have to go to the funeral to find out how it had happened.

The McGuires had many friends, Kessa thought as she walked down a street off Fifth Avenue to see a block-long line of limousines headed by a hearse. This was her first funeral. She had observed many corteges driving slowly through the streets of the city, but she had never known the passenger in the hearse before today.

Kessa forced herself to enter the funeral home. A directory in the lobby told her where to go: "Agustus ...... first floor. Thompson ...... second floor. McGuire ...... third floor"—as if they were parties for the living and not gatherings for the dead.

She slowly walked up the white marble staircase to the third floor. There, dozens of people were milling around and talking quietly in small groups. Then she saw the coffin. It was not dark-stained wood, as she expected, but white. And it was open. A gray-haired couple flanked by two young women, Deirdre's sisters, sat by the coffin. People approached them, shaking their hands solemnly or hugging them. Kessa edged toward them so she could overhear bits of greetings and comments made to the family.

"I'm so sorry."

"This must be terrible for you."

"It's such a shock."

"She was such a beautiful girl."

"She was a happy girl."

"I don't know what to say."

None of these remarks contained a clue as to how Deirdre had died.

Kessa watched an austere, middle-aged man walk away from the McGuires. He didn't seem to be in mourning. He must be the funeral director, Kessa decided, and he must know what was going on. She took a deep breath and decided to approach him.

"Excuse me."

He smiled politely at Kessa. "Yes, young lady?"

"I'm sorry to bother you, but do you know what kil—how Deirdre died?"

"I believe she died of anorexia nervosa, ultimately a heart attack. You know, many girls your age . . ."

"Thank you. I appreciate your clearing it up for me. Excuse me."

Kessa didn't care if he thought she was rude. She was in no mood for a lecture she thought as she walked rapidly out of the somber room. She pressed the elevator button, then turned around. She had to see Deirdre. She owed it to her friend.

As Kessa threaded her way back through the crowd, she realized she would have to greet the immediate family in order to get to the coffin. Once again, she took a deep breath.

"Mr. McGuire? My name is Kessa. I was Deirdre's friend. I called you on Saturday. I thought I should come today."

"Did you know her well?"

Kessa was surprised at the question. "Yes."

He hesitated. "Did you know how long she had been . . . doing that behavior?"

She knew he meant the vomiting. Why did he have to ask her that? She felt accused, as if she were an accomplice.

"No," she lied. "What behavior?"

"She had anorexia nervosa ... and apparently it contributed to her death. Thank you for your thoughtfulness in coming today."

Mr. McGuire turned to greet someone else.

Her heart thumping, Kessa edged toward the coffin. As she moved closer, each heartbeat seemed so intense that it hurt. She peered in. Deirdre, in a white lace dress, looked like she was sleeping. She was made up, and her mouth was slightly crooked. As she stared at her friend, tears welling in her eyes, Kessa overheard Mr. McGuire say to another man, "She broke off a front tooth. I guess she hit the toilet as she fell."

Kessa closed her eyes, but tears oozed out nonetheless. *As you hit the toilet*, she thought. She wanted to shout at her friend for dying over a toilet bowl. How could she die? It wasn't fair. It couldn't be true.

Kessa couldn't bear it. She nearly ran out of the funeral parlor. She crossed the street and stared at the line of black limousines. The hearse with the S-shaped chrome side braces on its canopylike top reminded her of a baby carriage.

She stayed there, not feeling the cold, not feeling anything, for nearly two hours. Finally, they came out. Six men carried the coffin, even whiter now in the bright sunlight, over to the back of the hearse. It rolled in effortlessly. They slammed the door behind it.

Everyone at school was talking about it. Groups of students clustered around their lunch trays in the cafeteria were mystified—and intimidated—by her death. Within days, Kessa could hear many of them joking, pointing to thin classmates and calling them anorexic. Within a week, everybody was kidding about it: "I wish I could get it for just a few weeks, so I could lose ten pounds." "Hey, you didn't eat your dessert. Are you getting anorexic or something?" Those students who remembered what had happened to Kessa kept away from her. They had to be able to joke about Deirdre's death because then they wouldn't think it was real. But Kessa made it real. Except she was still alive.

Kessa withdrew from her classmates and hurried out of the building as soon as the bell rang every afternoon. She'd walk aimlessly on the chic streets of the Upper East Side, lost in thought, still riddled with guilt. Sometimes she saw other thin girls who reminded her of Deirdre. Maybe it was their energetic gait or the toss of a head or the skinny dungareed legs that caused Kessa's heart to literally skip a beat. The skipped heartbeat fascinated her. Did that mean she'd have a heart attack like Deirdre? She wondered what death really meant. Where was Deirdre? Was she in heaven? Could she see Kessa? Once, Kessa even found herself stopping in the street, glancing at the sky and expecting to see her friend's face. How badly she wanted to talk to Deirdre. She'd shake her so hard and yell at her for being so stupid to die.

Then the image of Deirdre's face in her coffin—eyes closed, mouth a bit askew, skin pale and waxen—would fill Kessa's head. She hated that memory. It was proof that Deirdre was dead.

At one of her sessions she asked Sherman, "Do you believe in God?" Kessa had stated firmly that she didn't want to discuss Deirdre's death, so he had to keep his answer as nonspecific as her question.

"I'm never sure about that. Sometimes I find myself talking to the sky, though."

"Oh, I just don't understand how the dead body in a funeral parlor gets up to the sky," Kessa said blandly.

He watched the emotions on her face. She was trying so hard to feign detachment, as if they were having a philosophical discussion about no one in particular.

"That's why we call the dead body, as you put it, the remains. We assume that the spiritual being, as we knew it, has left the body."

Kessa looked down at the floor. Then where was Deirdre?

"I wish she hadn't died. I miss her," she whispered.

"Do you want to talk about it?"

"No!"

Talking about it would not bring Deirdre back.

Chapter
22

In the month following Deirdre's death, Kessa spent many extra hours in gymnastics and her weight went up to 110 pounds. But it was no reason to freak out, Kessa reasoned, because it was muscle weight, not fat. She just had to keep working out.

It was easiest for her to mingle with students in her gymnastics class. Nobody talked about anorexia. They just talked about the unevens and the beam and flips and leotards.

Kessa found herself drawn to the best gymnast in the class. Her name was Denise—Kessa was often tempted to call her Deirdre—but her nickname was Dennie. She was dark-haired, with broad shoulders and hips and well-muscled thighs, and she was an incorrigible flirt. She seemed completely at ease with guys, and Kessa sometimes wondered if she'd pick up any of Dennie's manner simply by being around her.

"Hey, you want to go out tonight?" Dennie asked her

during class when they were both spotting the unevens. "I'm sure we can scare up a couple of guys."

"Nice guys?"

"Yes, your highness, nice guys."

"Not dope dealers or junkies?"

"Boy Scounts can be arranged if you wish."

"Well, you know what I mean." Kessa blushed.

"What grade do you want them from?"

"Cut it out!" Kessa giggled.

When Dr. Gordon's office called to remind her that she had an appointment, Kessa felt guilty when she thought about all the fuss that had been made over her and her monthly check-ups while she was still alive and healthy and her friend was dead. Deirdre could have used some of that attention.

Dr. Gordon's office was bright and airy, its waiting room filled with toys and building blocks for children to play with. Kessa had been her patient from birth, so despite all the little kids in the waiting room, she always felt like she belonged.

Dr. Gordon stuck her head out of a doorway. "All right, Francesca. You're next, dear."

It was impossible to get angry with Dr. Gordon even if she always forgot to call her Kessa. Beneath her blustery facade, she was one of the most tender people Kessa had ever met. She had become a pediatrician with the hope that she wouldn't have to do painful things to children or to see them when they were severely ill. She liked well-baby check-ups the best and she couldn't bear to see children with fatal diseases, so she limited her hospital involvement and turned over patients with severe diseases to Dr. Donaldson, who thrived on the challenge to heal those sick children.

As Kessa walked past several of the examining rooms, she

recalled the terror she'd felt on previous visits, when she'd hoped Dr. Gordon wouldn't notice she was continually losing weight. Kessa stopped for a moment, thinking that she was to enter the purple room. Each room had a color-coded door.

"No, Francesca, all the examining rooms are filled. I just thought I'd rescue you from the two-year-old terrors in the waiting room. You can sit in my consulting room while we wait for a vacancy."

"Sounds good to me. Take your time, Dr. Gordon."

"Should I be insulted?".

"No. I just wouldn't want you to rush on my account."

"See ya soon, dear," Dr. Gordon said as she went into the red room.

Kessa sat down in front of the modern Danish desk and looked around the office. The blond-wood shelves held small statues next to framed photos of Dr. Gordon's husband and two daughters. Dr. Gordon was proud of them and was quick to tell anyone who commented on the photos that one daughter was also a doctor and the other a lawyer. Kessa noticed the file folders on the desk. She thought it might be fun to snoop and see what the doctors had written about her when she'd been in the hospital.

Sure enough, right on the top she found FRANCESCA LOUISE DIETRICH. She was about to open the folder when she noticed another file on the right side of the desk. It was labeled DEIRDRE AINSLY MCGUIRE. Kessa's heart began to thump. She leaned over the desk and stared at the report cover. *Deirdre*. She looked up at the door. It was closed. She sat down in Dr. Gordon's chair, took a deep breath, and opened the file. AUTOPSY REPORT, it said in bold type. Kessa's eyes watered, and she felt dizzy. She blinked rapidly. Slowly, the words swam into focus.

> I performed an autopsy of *McGuire, Deirdre Ainsly*, at the DEPARTMENT OF CHIEF MEDICAL EXAMINER-CORONER, New York County, New York, on October 20th, at 20:48 hours.
>
> From the anatomical findings and pertinent history, I ascribe the death to: HYPOKALEMIA . . . DUE TO OR AS A CONSEQUENCE OF: ANOREXIA NERVOSA/HYPER-EMESIS.

She turned the pages, past the charts containing the results of the laboratory tests and blood samples she didn't comprehend. Finally, she came to a page she could understand.

> The body is clothed in a red blouse with white buttons down the front, and black slacks. The blouse contains stains, which appear to be vomitus. The body measures . . .

The dizziness returned, and Kessa skipped down the page, not knowing what she was looking for. Two phrases caught her eye.

> The toenails contained pink polish.
> The brain weighs 1185 grams.

She quickly flipped to the next page and hurriedly scanned it, reading only the large type.

There was a paragraph after each title:

"HEART: The heart weighs 185 grams.

"RESPIRATORY SYSTEM: The right lung weighs 420 grams. The left lung weighs 412 grams.

"LIVER: The liver weighs 1730 grams.

"BLADDER: empty."

The list went on until all the organs were accounted for.
Kessa couldn't read anymore.

"The brain weighs 1185 grams."

She straightened out the papers and closed the folder, sat
back in the swivel chair to catch her breath, and stared up at
Dr. Gordon's fluorescent light. The door opened.

"So you want to play doctor, eh?" Dr. Gordon said almost
teasingly. "Well, we'll just have to give you a stethoscope to
go with the office."

Kessa managed a smile, which took nearly all of her will
power.

"In the meantime, while you're waiting for your degree,
you'll have to remain the patient. Come, my dear. The
examining room awaits you, but from your looks you don't
need it."

Kessa followed Dr. Gordon down the brightly lit hallway
to the yellow door. As she entered, she wondered what the
examining room in the morgue looked like. Was it yellow,
too? Or purple or red, like blood? Did Deirdre bleed when
they cut her open?

"How fast can you get out of your clothes? We can make
this quick." Dr. Gordon's voice cut into her thoughts.

"One second!"

Kessa pulled off her sweater and turtleneck together and
unzipped and jumped out of her jeans in what looked like a
single motion.

"I'm really impressed! Anyone who can move that fast
must be suffering from good health. But I'm supposed to
examine you anyway. This shouldn't be a big deal, Francesca. I'm just going to poke your belly and check your liver,
spleen, and digestive tract. At the worst, it'll tickle."

Kessa lay on the examining table, trying to imagine the
autopsy. She closed her eyes.

"Not ticklish today?"

Kessa shrugged.

"Okay. Sit up while I listen to your heart and lungs."

Kessa felt the cold stethoscope on her back.

"Now take a deep breath." Dr. Gordon walked around in front of her and placed the stethoscope on her chest.

"That's quite a heartbeat! You weren't doing push-ups in my office for the past ten minutes, were you?"

"Oh no, the past ten years!" Kessa tried to joke. "But I still get nervous for these check-ups," she lied.

"That's odd. You never seemed this nervous when you were worried about my putting you in the hospital last spring."

"I was a better liar last spring," she lied again.

"Well, it's good to have the real Francesca back again."

That was the worst thing to say. "*I hate the* real *Francesca!*" Kessa wanted to shout. "*She'll never be back!*" She turned her head to the wall.

Dr. Gordon noticed the gesture. "You *are* back, aren't you dear?"

"I'm here, Dr. Gordon."

"You sure have something on your mind. I hope he's handsome."

"He is!" Kessa jumped at the excuse.

"Well, he must be something. Your blood pressure's up to normal, which is a lot higher than it was a few months ago."

"Then you won't have to send me back to the hospital and I won't need those injections and they won't have to stick that tube back in that vein in my chest! They won't all stand around looking at my body like that and stitch the tube in again?"

Dr. Gordon was stunned by the accelerating intensity of Kessa's questions. The girl was nearly hysterical.

"Francesca!" She placed her hands on Kessa's shoulders. "What's the matter? You know that's all over."

"Deirdre's dead!" Kessa cried, and broke into sobs.

Dr. Gordon went white as she realized that Kessa had been sitting behind her desk. She might have seen the autopsy report.

"What were you doing behind my desk, Francesca?"

"Reading her goddamn autopsy report!" Kessa shouted between sobs.

Dr. Gordon pulled her close, tears filling her own eyes, and rocked her gently until Kessa cried herself out.

"They only buried her face, her arms, and her legs," Kessa said in a muffled voice, her face still resting on Dr. Gordon's shoulder.

Dr. Gordon held the girl tightly, patted her gently on the back, the way she would a frightened young child. "Oh, Francesca, you should never read any autopsy report. They're all grotesque." Her voice choked to a whisper. "But above all, not a report on a person you knew and cared about and laughed with. Even we folks in the white coats try to stay away from those."

"But you don't understand. I knew what she was doing. I could have stopped her!" Kessa couldn't stop shivering.

"I don't think you could have stopped her. I'm sure she didn't ask you to. Did she?"

"No. She wouldn't even let me talk about it with her . . . " Kessa's voice trailed off.

"Then how could you take responsibility for her?"

"I was her friend. I should have been able to do something. I knew what it was like. It's as if her life slipped through my fingers while I just stood there and watched."

"We hate how helpless we are when we see someone that we care about destroy herself." Dr. Gordon paused. She needed to keep her voice calm. "I hated watching you lose pound after pound and I didn't even know what to say to you that would make a difference, that would stop you before you damaged or killed yourself. And I was the one your mother was counting on, Francesca. I was the *doctor*, and I was helpless."

"I didn't know you were struggling through all that when I was sick. I'm sorry," Kessa said, hugging her doctor tightly. "You see, I'm totally useless. I make people around me miserable, and I couldn't even help my friend who had the same problem I had . . . and still have . . . a little."

"Francesca my dear, you must believe that may, at times, make you the person *least* qualified to help."

"Why?"

"It's always tricky to help a friend with an emotional problem. You need lots of knowledge, and you also need something you didn't have—distance—so you know where she ends and you begin. Helping her is different from going down with her. It's a terrible shame. You had the knowledge—I sure didn't—and I had the distance. And in the end Deirdre still had the power to destroy herself."

"I still don't understand why she died."

"Hypokalemia means that Deirdre kept binge eating and vomiting until she lost so much potassium—that's one of the chemicals that connects our nerves—until the electrical connections in her body were short-circuited and her heart lost its rhythm."

"So if she hadn't done all that vomiting she wouldn't have died?"

"Probably not."

Kessa began crying again, with what little energy she had left.

"Then it's still my fault."

"Francesca, I just explained to you—we don't have that kind of power over our friends."

"No, I could have done more. The night she died I had asked her to go out with me. We went to Skirmishes. It's a bar. We were going to try to pick up some guys—as an experiment. I was scared, but I lied and pretended that I wasn't. Deirdre was more scared than I was. She left. I could have stopped her. I could have followed her. I could have *not* asked her to come with me that night, and then she wouldn't have gotten upset enough to go home and eat and throw up."

Dr. Gordon gently loosened their embrace and put her hand on Kessa's chin, tilting her head so she could look her straight in the eye.

"Now look, Francesca. Even if you had lived with Deirdre, you would have had a very tough time stopping her even once. I think you're going to have to accept your helplessness just like the rest of us."

Kessa thought again of the day in the girls' room when Deirdre had pushed her out of the way and thrown up in front of her. She took a deep breath. "Why do we do that? Why do we do such crazy stuff?"

"I wish I were smart enough to know, Francesca."

"I love you, Dr. Gordon."

Evelyn Gordon's eyes filled. She hugged Kessa again, partly out of affection and partly to hide her own tears.

Chapter
23

Kessa left Dr. Gordon's office and walked slowly uptown, eyeing other teenage girls who passed by. They made her jealous—they looked so casual, so outgoing, so carefree. Why had she fallen into the "trap" of anorexia, as Sandy Sherman had called it. She infuriated herself. The voice in her head that used to scream "You're too fat!" was still there, but most of the time it remained a taunting whisper. It only became louder when she was tired or angry or frightened. Most of the time at school, she was able to talk to girls her own age—make friends—without feeling that an immeasurable gulf separated them.

As she wandered up Second Avenue, she looked at the chic restaurants with their glassed-in seating areas, reminiscent of the sidewalk cafes she'd seen in Paris when her parents took her there many years ago. Everyone was constantly meeting around food. Her friends were always making suggestions. "Do you want to meet for lunch?" or "Let's get together for coffee" or "Want to try a new restaurant up the street?" She declined all invitations around food, except for when she'd gone with Deirdre for pizza—and look what had happened then. Though Kessa was no longer starving herself, she did maintain intensive control over what she ate, planning her days around eating: the time of each meal or snack, what it was, how much of it to eat. She would politely refuse dates if they interfered with these routines, even though she'd get a twinge of nervousness whenever she did so, fearing she might return to the old pattern of unstoppable weight loss.

Kessa remembered the hospital. Looking up at the doctors, three men who had seemed huge and scary, who threaded a plastic tube through her chest, down six inches to her jugular vein. Then they turned on the fluids—two thousand calories a day, coursing into her body, making her fat! Lila couldn't believe that Kessa would endure surgery just because she refused to eat. Lila and the hospital. She knew she'd probably never see Lila again, in the park or anywhere. And she'd never, ever see Deirdre again. How she wished someone had hospitalized Deirdre.

Kessa passed a coffee shop and noticed two girls sitting together, laughing as they sipped hot chocolate. Girls from her school. She ducked her head but took a quick, intense look in their direction, more to remember clearly what she had seen than to be noticed by them. It made her angry and jealous that they could sit and talk so easily over food, so she decided to call Dennie and meet her for coffee. She looked at her watch. It was nearly time for her appointment with Sandy Sherman. Two doctors in one day! As she made her way to Sherman's office, she forced herself to look into the windows of all the restaurants she passed—Italian, Thai, Japanese, Chinese, Hungarian, seafood, pizza, even the nondescript coffee shops—over and over, to intensify her anger at being excluded.

By the time Kessa entered Sherman's office, she was ready to blow up.

After greeting her in the waiting room with his usual "Kessa, come in," Sandy turned to her as she took her seat and asked, "What's the matter?"

"You mean it shows that much?"

"If you're bothered, it's supposed to show. Especially here."

"Well, I'm plenty bothered ... about a lot of things. Being a failure!" Kessa started to cry. "I failed to keep Deirdre alive! I never stop thinking about her."

Sandy waited quietly until Kessa took several tissues and blew her nose in the same unobtrusive way she did most things. He struggled to find the right words. He didn't want to speak too soon, but he also didn't want to leave her with a silence that would make her feel ignored.

"You never wanted to talk about that before."

"There are things I hate to even think about."

"About Deirdre?"

Kessa stared out the window.

"How did she die?" Sandy asked softly.

She continued to stare blankly even though tears trickled down her cheeks.

"Do you miss her?"

The vacant look was immediately replaced by an angry terror. "She was just like me! It could have been me!"

"It could have been." He nodded.

"She's always in my mind. Sometimes I think I see her in the street. Other times I remember her funeral ... her autopsy."

"Her autopsy?" Sherman couldn't keep the surprise out of his voice.

"I, uh, found the report on Dr. Gordon's desk and read

some of it. Most of it. Do you know what they did to her?" Kessa demanded.

"Do you want to tell me?"

"They took out her brain. They weighed it." Her jaw was clenched, her mouth tight. "Then they cut it up!" She took a deep breath. "They did that to every bit of her insides. They rummaged around inside of her the way shoppers might look at a pile of scarves on sale. They wrote down everything. They said her bladder was empty!" She stopped, overwhelmed again by sobs.

"Whenever I think about it, I imagine it's me on that slab. I see them reaching inside of me, taking out my heart and my lungs. It's disgusting! It's humiliating! I should never have let her leave Skirmishes that night! That was the night she died. Maybe if we'd stayed together that night, she would still be alive. I know that I couldn't stop her from doing that crazy eating, but just that night, if she weren't so alone, it wouldn't have been so bad and she would have made it through."

"Feeling guilty can be a way to escape your feelings of powerlessness."

Kessa's eyes narrowed. That was not what she wanted to hear. She remained in an angry silence for a long minute.

"I'm powerless about everything! And with everybody!"

"No you're not. But you were for a while."

"When?"

"When all your thoughts were about eating and weight."

Kessa slowly felt the anger ebb out of her body. "When will it ever be all gone?"

"Eventually. Gradually. When we learn to hurt in one style, we let go of it very slowly and we can temporarily be pushed back into it if life plays enough bad tricks on us at once. But it's just the flavor that returns—not the problem."

"But it's still there," Kessa sighed. "Sometimes I feel like

I'm so locked out. It's still so hard to talk to people. I can't eat with them, so the more I drift away, the more I get afraid of what they'll think of me and the more I withdraw."

"What does eating with them have to do with talking with them?"

"*Are you kidding*! When else do people get together, unless they're working or in school, except to eat? When do you get together with *your* friends?"

"I guess I'm not on the ball today. You're right. So you're mad at yourself for having to live by the rules?"

"I'm beginning to hate living by the rules. On days when I'm feeling up, I can forget most of them. But on days when I'm down, I drown in them."

"What determines an up day or a down day?"

"Whether I feel fat or not."

"What determines whether you feel fat or not?"

"Whether I'm fat . . . or not." She started to giggle.

"Do you have two wardrobes—still? One for fat days and one for 'not' days?"

"Well, I know it sounds silly, but I wear baggy clothes on days when I feel fat."

"You keep saying 'I feel fat,' so I assume you know that you aren't really fat on days you *feel* fat."

"Sort of. I mean, it isn't like it used to be. It's funny. When I wasn't this fat, I used to feel fatter. Now that I'm the heaviest I've been in a year and a half, I never get as upset as when I was twenty-five pounds lighter."

Sandy picked up his cup of coffee, took a sip, and put it back down. Kessa peered at his cup, noting the light color of the coffee and two empty sugar wrappers that lay on his desk.

"See, even you do it."

"Do what?"

"Eat, or at least drink, when we talk."

"Let's back up a little. What you're telling me is that you're beginning to hate something even worse than fat: loneliness."

"But it's the 'fat' thoughts that keep me lonely."

"There was a time when you would never refer to these ideas as 'fat thoughts.' You would shout at me about how fat you really were."

"Well, now I know I'm not fat . . . sometimes. Will I always have to feel this way?"

"Has it changed in the past year?"

"Of course."

"Then why not assume that in the coming year it'll continue to change at the same rate."

"That would be great," Kessa mused. "At this rate, in another year I'd be nearly free." She looked at his coffee again. "How much milk and sugar do you put in your coffee, anyway?"

"Oh, about a pint of heavy cream and a pound of sugar. Hey, you're not going to switch from fear of your becoming fat to fear of *me* becoming fat, are you?"

"It's a temptation. Then I could yell at you instead of me." She smiled.

Grinning back, Sandy patted his stomach. "Go right ahead, but I won't listen to your orders the way you listen to your own. In fact, I'll probably ignore them entirely."

"I'm going to call Dennie," Kessa decided. "I met her in gymnastics. It's been lonely without Deirdre . . ." Her voice trailed off.

He waited.

"But Dennie's okay. I think she's black. It's hard to tell, because she's so light. She's a good gymnast and she weighs more than me, but she isn't fat. Anyway, I'm going to ask her to have lunch with me. She even makes boys sound safe. So I guess food will be okay."

"I was wondering about what else isn't safe for you. You've mentioned food and boys. What about talk?"

"What do you mean?"

"You don't really say a lot here. You've almost always given me the briefest answers and the shortest sentences. It sometimes seems that you have to rehearse everything in your head before you say it—to me, at least. It seems that you're afraid of rambling, of thinking out loud, of unrehearsed talk—careless talk that might be full of mistakes—or disclosures you're not sure you want to make. I know you've yelled in here and that's been spontaneous, but that's only when you couldn't keep it in anymore. Even those outbursts have been brief. Why are you so careful with your talk?"

Kessa shrugged. "It's like eating in front of someone. I feel exposed. When I eat in front of people, I wonder if they're going to think I'm a pig or something."

"How does that connect up with your fear of talking?"

"I never know if they're going to think I'm foolish. Some people always know what to say. I'm not one of them."

"So you remain brief with people?"

"I guess I'm what you call a good listener. I think people like me better for it."

"It sounds like your main concern is what others think of you."

"I don't know if it's others or me—what I think of myself," Kessa said carefully.

"There's a way to tell which it is."

"How?"

"Has anyone accused you of eating like a pig?"

"No."

"Has anyone ever told you that you sound foolish or boring when you talk to them?"

"No." Kessa looked at the floor.

"Are you just as careful when no one's around as when you're with people?"

"Maybe. Almost."

Sandy sat, watching her carefully. Though the silence in the room was uncomfortable, it wasn't hostile. Kessa began to fidget. Sandy picked up his coffee again and slurped it loudly. At first she looked annoyed, but then she smiled. Her grin quickly faded when she realized she understood what Sandy meant. "So you mean that I've invented everyone's attitude toward me?"

"If you have no evidence that the criticism really exists, it sounds like you're being unnecessarily tough on yourself."

"Why do I have to do that?"

"You don't know another way to feel safe—although you're questioning it so much now that I guess you're learning that 'invented' safety isn't so great."

"Didn't you worry about what I'd think when you slurped your coffee?"

"I'm glad you noticed. I confess that I did it to provoke you."

"How could you not worry about what someone else thinks?"

"Kessa, all of us do some worrying about what others think of us. What varies is the *degree* to which we're concerned. How much do you worry about what others think of you?"

"As much as possible."

"But you don't seem to *know* anyone else. You have a difficult time making eye contact. How could you know what anybody's thinking about you if you can't even look at their face?"

"What if I don't like what I see?"

"Then ask, 'What's the matter?' and see what he says— or she says."

"But who am I to ask what's the matter? I mean, maybe I'm making a nerd out of myself. I don't want someone to think I'm a jerk."

"I think what you're telling me is that you feel that people around you are very powerful."

She nodded, looking awkward. "Everybody but my parents. I don't think they're powerful."

"How about me?"

"What do you mean?"

"Am I powerful?"

She smiled shyly. "Yeah, but you're *friendly* powerful—most of the time."

"Then you must feel unprotected nearly all the time, since you have no powerful allies in your life."

"Except here—and maybe with Dennie. But she's new."

"What about Deirdre?"

"She was like a sicker version of me. I can always feel powerful if I hang around people who seem like me but are in more trouble than I am. When I help them, sometimes I pretend that someone like me is helping me—I pretend I'm them."

"But Dennie doesn't feel like that to you?"

"No. I want to be like her."

"Then copy her until it's you."

"If she keeps liking me."

"You're definitely likable. Just don't try too hard. And make more eye contact with her than you make with me!"

Kessa opened her eyes so wide she thought they'd burst. "Yes, sir!"

Chapter
24

Eye contact, Kessa murmured to herself as she walked to catch the crosstown bus. *Look* at people. She realized that she rarely ever actually *looked* at people, noticing their clothes, their habits, the expressions on their faces. The whole world was out there and she hadn't been paying any attention at all. Now that was going to change.

First she concentrated on taking in the whole street: the traffic, cabs and cars honking; the two-story buildings housing European designers; the long shadows cast by everyone on this late autumn afternoon; the faces of people walking toward her. For the first time, she looked at their faces. *Really* looked. If anyone returned her glance, she turned her head . . . toward the next face coming her way.

The faces weren't very open at this time of day: working mothers were rushing home with the groceries they'd purchased as they got off the bus; businessmen seemed weary as they came out of the subway. She'd chosen a good time to "face-watch," Kessa thought, since most of her subjects were too preoccupied to notice that they were being studied by a very shy girl.

"Hello there!" one man flirted back. Kessa ignored him. Another man tried to stare her down. It made her smile. Suddenly Madison Avenue had become a sea of faces and all that mattered was to look at them. Look and learn. Not until Kessa boarded the crosstown bus and the driver loudly said, "Fare, please," did she return to her habitual self-consciousness.

"Oh sure. Sorry." She was almost angry that he had interrupted her reverie, the most unself-conscious few minutes she could ever remember. For the rest of the trip home, she worried as usual about the glances of others.

The phone rang five times before someone answered, and Kessa nearly hung up. "Who's there?" a stern voice demanded.

"This is Kessa. I go to school with Dennie. May I please speak with her?"

She heard the woman shout, "Denise!" but then she must have put her hand over the mouthpiece because Kessa didn't hear anything until Dennie picked up the phone.

"Hi, Kessa?"

"Did I call at a bad time? I can call back later."

"Yeah—yes. We're setting up for dinner now. Could I call you back at nine?"

Dennie didn't have the confident, light-hearted tone she used in school. She sounded rushed, nervous, and apologetic.

"Sure! I'll be home. 'Bye." Kessa hung up. She played no role in "setting up" dinner in her home—except as inspector, to see if the food was to her liking. From just that short conversation, Kessa sensed that Dennie was intimidated by her mother. That was pretty ironic. Kessa's mother seemed pretty intimidated by her own daughter.

As if on cue, Kessa heard her mother call, "Harold, Kessa! Dinner's on."

Kessa entered the dining room from the kitchen, circling around the table to see what her mother had prepared.

Harold sat down, drink in hand, slightly annoyed as usual by his daughter's inspection. He gave her the once-over, then forgot his annoyance. He was secretly delighted with Kessa's changed appearance—not only her weight gain, but the muscles shaped by gymnastics. Hal Dietrich had no use for skinny or soft people—men or women.

"Kessa, you're looking good these days."

She frowned. "You mean I look fat," she mumbled.

"No, damnit. I don't mean fat. I mean strong, healthy. Is it important for you to have me hate the way you look? You certainly act that way."

She didn't answer. Grace came in with a tureen of soup. "It's soup season," she announced with conspicuous cheerfulness.

"That's the best part of fall—cold weather cooking. What kind of soup is it, Grace?"

"Homemade carrot and rice."

This good food conversation made Kessa sulk. She hated it—pointed, as it was, awkwardly at her.

"Sounds good to me," Kessa said with forced enthusiasm. Her moods still dominated the table. She looked across the table at her father, who now avoided her eyes, and she began to feel sorry for him. He looked upset. Why was it all so complicated?

At nine o'clock the phone rang. Kessa had been staring at it and she grabbed the receiver.

"Dennie?"

"How'd you know it was me?"

"You said you'd call back at nine. Your mother sounded

sort of annoyed before. Is she strict about your getting calls at dinnertime?"

"I'll tell you about that some other time." Dennie's voice sounded forced.

Kessa cleared her throat. "Would you like to meet me for lunch this Saturday? I thought we might go to this café on Second Avenue."

Dennie hesitated. Again Kessa thought how different she sounded at home. "Sounds great, but I'll have to ask my mother. Could you hold on a minute?"

"Oh sure."

Kessa heard Dennie put down the phone and walk into another room. She couldn't hear any of the words, but from the sounds and inflections of their voices, it seemed that Dennie was having a hard time. Kessa started to feel nervous. Maybe this wasn't such a good idea after all. If Dennie's mom got mad, then Dennie would blame Kessa and she wouldn't want to be friends . . .

"Kessa?"

"Yes, I'm here."

"Oh, sorry to take so long, but I had to change stuff around for the day. It's okay now."

"Great. Could you meet me on the corner of Seventy-second and Second at eleven-thirty, and we'll walk down. The place is only about ten minutes from there. It's called Café des Amis. You'll love it."

"Okay. See you in school tomorrow. 'Bye." She hung up.

Kessa was baffled by the whole conversation. Perhaps Dennie was uncomfortable talking on the phone. And she wondered what Dennie's mom was like. Was the fearless, self-assured Dennie actually afraid of her own mother?

Chapter
25

Kessa paced in a small circle at the corner of Seventy-second and Second Avenue. It was a busy corner, with trucks and cars headed downtown and taxis racing around them. It was eleven forty-eight. Dennie was eighteen minutes late. Kessa looked up from her watch for the hundredth time to see Dennie walking nonchalantly toward her.

"Did you get stuck on a train?" Kessa tried hard to hide her anxiety.

"What do you mean?"

"You're a little late. I thought maybe you had trouble getting here."

Dennie looked down at her own watch. "Kessa, you must live by a stopwatch or something. This isn't late."

"Well, I just thought that we should get seated by noon."

"Or we change into pumpkins?" Dennie laughed.

"It's hard to get a table after noon," Kessa said lamely.

"Hey, c'mon. It's Saturday. There's no rush. I didn't think we were meeting 'cause we're hungry. It's 'cause we wanted to get together to talk, right?"

Kessa tensed up immediately. Now Dennie was going to think she was weird. She was just making too much of her noontime eating ritual.

They started to walk down Second Avenue. "So where is this restaurant you like so much?" Dennie asked as she paused to look in the window of a shoe store. "God, those shoes are expensive."

"I've never eaten there myself, but I've been told that it's really good. I passed it the other day and it looked chic, so I thought it would be fun for us to eat there."

"Ah! This is an experiment, then!"

Kessa got even more nervous. How could Dennie know that this was an experiment? "What do you mean?"

"Kessa, you're so funny. Why do you look so serious?"

"I don't know. I guess I wouldn't want to take you to a lousy restaurant."

Dennie pointed. "Is that it? Up ahead on the right?"

Kessa replied, "Yeah. Café des Amis."

Dennie shrugged. "It looks expensive. We better check out the menu in the window so we don't have to wash dishes."

They approached the glassed-in eating area that spilled out onto the sidewalk, and scanned the menu. "It's not so bad for lunch," Dennie said, relief in her voice as she pushed the heavy wooden door open.

Kessa waited for Dennie to choose a table, then sat down opposite her. Dennie glanced around at the hanging plants, the brass candlesticks, and the folded linen napkins with a funny look on her face.

"Haven't you ever been to one of these places before?" Kessa asked.

"No. I'm not your typical private-school kid."

Kessa bit her lip.

"Because I'm black and not rich."

Kessa blushed crimson. "I'm—"

"Black and not rich too?" Dennie broke into laughter.

Kessa smiled in relief. Dennie didn't hate her after all. "I just feel awkward about that," she replied.

"I guess I made you feel awkward, Kessa. I suppose if I succeed in making everyone feel awkward, I'm going to be pretty lonely at school. People keep at arm's length from me for enough of the superficial reasons. I don't want you to back off."

"But, Dennie, you always seem comfortable in school. I really envy how comfortable you seem with everybody, boys or girls."

Dennie gave a short laugh. "When you think you've gotten to some place you don't belong, you feel like any minute they're all going to notice you, so you act confident, like you want to tell people you don't care. I guess I want to tell myself that I don't care, either."

Kessa was about to respond when the waiter approached the table to take their order. "Do you ladies know what you'd like? Or would you like to look at the menu?"

The girls looked at each other, then Dennie smiled at the waiter. "Could you bring us menus, please?"

"Sure," he responded cheerfully as he poured water into their glasses, then dashed off to his station, where he grabbed two leatherbound menus and brought them back to the table with a flourish.

Kessa sat very still until he left them alone.

"I think you can talk now!" Dennie giggled.

Kessa made a face. She hadn't realized her feelings were quite so transparent, even though Sandy had told her he often guessed what she was thinking from the look on her face.

"Waiters always make me feel uncomfortable," she

admitted. "I feel like they're waiting for me to do something stupid."

"I don't get it. You're white and you belong wherever you go, but you're always worried about what everybody thinks of you. What do you think they'll do to you?"

Kessa shook her head. "You must think I'm pretty weird, but I don't ever feel like I belong and I don't even know why I feel that way. Someone once told me that maybe I never felt like I belonged in my family."

Dennie smiled. "It's just the opposite for me. I know I belong in my family. I just may not belong anywhere else. I mean, we fight all the time in my family, but everyone always knows that when push comes to shove, we're all we've got."

"No, it's totally different for me," Kessa said. "When my sister Suzanna's home—my brother Gregg's almost never there at all, and I've written him off anyway, because he only cares about himself—when the four of us are together it feels like we're all checking up on each other to see who's gyping whom. I don't know who my parents believe's on their side, but when I'm home, I feel like nobody's safe."

"Maybe it *is* harder for you, then. See, for me, everyone outside of my family is the enemy, or potential enemy anyway. What does your family worry about? Or who?"

"I think we just worry about each other. It never seems like we have anybody else to worry about."

"You know, my mother once said that the further people get from worrying about survival, the more screwed up they get. She said that's because we don't know what's supposed to be important once we get our basic act together."

Kessa was startled. She had never thought to quote her own mother to a friend.

"Your mother sounds pretty smart . . . and strong. That

must feel good to you."

"My mother is one tough, beautiful lady. I want to be like her, but I'd like to have it easier. I either won't have kids— but I doubt that—or I'll only marry someone who's totally crazy about me."

"Why do you say that? Aren't you looking for someone to fall in love with?"

"I wish it worked that way. My mom says that that's what guys are always into—who turns them on, who they fall in love with. The next thing you know is that it's no longer you—it's someone else! Then you've got three kids you have to bring up yourself."

"Is that what happened to your mom?"

"I didn't read about it in a book," Dennie said without bitterness, as if she were confiding in Kessa, sharing a secret bit of inherited wisdom. And she'd quoted her mother again. Kessa still couldn't get over that. She definitely had to meet Dennie's mom. "Do you think that we could get together at each other's houses?"

Dennie looked hesitant. She fiddled with the sugar, which made Kessa nervous. They'd have to order soon.

"I don't know how it is with your parents, but my mother isn't so crazy about having, uh, white people up to the apartment."

"I don't understand. She lets you go to school with us. I mean, a Manhattan private school is a lot whiter than a Manhattan public school."

"That's different. It's opportunity. I'm allowed to be edu- cated with white students, especially in a top-notch private school, because that'll really help for college admission and jobs later on."

"So why not friendships?" Kessa pressed her.

"It's hard. You know how light I am. I can almost pass for white . . . but luckily, I can't quite do it. You can really tell

I'm not."

Kessa must have looked confused, because Dennie smiled and explained. "If you're black but you can pass for white, you have to hear all kinds of antiblack wisecracks. But if people *see* that you're black, they're polite and you don't have to listen to that stuff."

Kessa felt more embarrassed than ever. She didn't know what to say, so she glanced down at the menu, immediately searching out the diet section. She wondered if Dennie really hated her for being white.

Dennie berated herself as she read her menu. She hadn't meant to get so heavy-duty with Kessa.

"What are you going to order?" Kessa looked up first.

"Just some soup and a hamburger. How 'bout you?"

Kessa stared at the menu again. If she ordered a salad, she was afraid Dennie would be critical, but she was too tense to really eat anything. Then she spotted the perfect compromise. "I'll have the chef's salad," she said with a sigh of relief. It looked substantial, but she could pick at it without really eating anything too fattening.

"Listen, I'm sorry I laid all that guilt trip on you."

"That's all right. I'm sorry your mom won't let me meet her."

"Hey, don't jump to conclusions. Sometimes I go overboard. I'll let you know." Dennie leaned back and smiled. "So. Enough of this family bullshit. Tell me who you think is cute, and I'll probably tell you he's a jerk."

Chapter
26

The late afternoon light cast deep shadows in the courtyard, but total darkness was still a month away. Kessa knew the sun's habits in that courtyard after more than a year of therapy.

"Not eating your lunch calmed you down?"

"Not really. I hoped it would. I didn't feel as if I had a choice."

Sherman felt a momentary twinge of deep anxiety about the possibility of Kessa starting to lose weight again. He weighed his words carefully. "I guess at that time you didn't have any choice emotionally."

"What's that supposed to mean? Am I going to be ano-rectic forever? Maybe I don't look it, but it's still there inside. Why do I have to be so rigid with myself? All these messages I give myself to control eating and exercise and weight. I don't want to feel this way for the rest of my life."

"Is it as strong as it used to be?"

She shot a defiant look in his direction. "Yes!" Then she shrugged and shook her head. "I don't know, damnit!" she yelled. "I guess it's less strong than it used to be. I can eat enough to pass..." Dennie's remarks about passing for white flashed through her mind. "But when I succeed in passing, I feel like a fraud. When I hear people talking about how I used to be or I hear them commenting about some weird anorectic they've seen, I get mad and want to yell, 'I'm still one of them, so shut up!' "

"What does it mean to you to still be one of them?"

"It means that I still feel driven to do the same things that 'they' do ... and that I'm just as crazy as they are."

Her words reverberated in the room. Kessa blew her nose. Her last statement sounded overly extreme even to her.

"Kessa, do you know what a setback is?"

"I don't know what you mean."

"Sometimes when you make a lot of progress but something scary happens one day, you're transported back to your worst feelings. You feel like you did the first week in the hospital."

She nodded.

"It doesn't mean that you haven't made real progress. It means that the change you made is new and fragile and that if you're pushed too hard, you'll hurt in the way you were used to hurting and you'll fight that hurt in the way you used to fight it."

She looked surprised, then thoughtful. "So what happens next? Does it go away?"

"You don't really think that it will go away, do you? You feel like you're back where you started." He winked.

"How long does it take to go away?"

"There's no way to predict. Usually, between a half day and several days, depending on how bad the scare was and how long it lasted."

"Will I always want to lose weight when I get scared?"

"I don't think so. But the ghost of that desire lingers for a long time and fades slowly."

"So I have to learn that it's a ghost? Does that mean I'm haunted?" Kessa tried to joke.

"Yes." Sandy smiled mischievously. "And that it will haunt you for a while."

"But it can't drag me all the way back forever?"

"Not if we don't let it."

The school cafeteria was always crowded, even though many students ate out. If they didn't brown-bag it, they took a chance at the steam table, hoping to avoid the worst of the overdone meatloaf and soggy canned vegetables.

Dennie sauntered up to Kessa, who was waiting on line, with a huge smile on her face. "Hey, girl, wanna eat at this restaurant together?"

"Sure, what the heck. I'm stuck here anyway, and there aren't any waiters."

"Kessa, I spoke to my mom and she wants you to have dinner with us."

Kessa was both delighted and panic-stricken—delighted to meet Dennie's mother, but panic-stricken because it was around food. It was always around food. Kessa couldn't keep her fears off her face. Dennie took a look and decided that her offer was being rejected.

"Hey, are you interested or—"

"Sure," Kessa interrupted. "I want to meet your mom. I was just surprised."

"I thought maybe you changed your mind or something."

"No, that's not it at all. You see, I have this problem with eating. I get self-conscious about it."

"Is that why you didn't eat when we were at, um—whatchamacallit's—Café des Amis?"

"You noticed?"

"At those prices, are you kidding!"

They both started laughing.

"Look, you can come over for a cup of coffee . . . corn flakes."

"God, how can I turn such a fabulous offer down?"

Kessa kept laughing. She'd never been teased like that about her eating before. And she'd never been able to laugh back. Maybe, she told herself, just maybe I'm really getting better.

They boarded the uptown express train at 86th and Lexington, grabbing seats right away. Kessa had only been on the subway once since she began high school—her parents decided it was too dangerous, and she was told to ride the buses—so she felt a little apprehensive even though she was with Dennie. She tried to appraise each passenger in the car. She decided that the women in her car weren't going to be dangerous, but a group of girls might be. She watched four girls, clad in uniforms of tight jeans, colored sneakers, and high school letter jackets, standing in the corner of the car laughing and joking above the roar of the train. Though their loudness frightened her, their obvious camaraderie made her jealous. They chewed gum vigorously, screamed in amusement at some shared joke, and even smacked each other, all in good humor. Dennie gave the girls a quick glance, then frowned at the floor. Kessa was confused. Why would Dennie disapprove?

The graffiti-covered train roared further uptown into Harlem, its fluorescent lights flickering. Almost all of the remaining passengers were black or Hispanic, and Kessa was feeling terribly white and conspicuous even though nobody was paying any real attention to them. The men in the car seemed weary and disinterested. The women remained alert, as though they might have to defend themselves. Kessa was already dreading the trip home. Maybe she'd call a cab.

She stole a glance at the four girls. They were looking at her and Dennie, giggling and cracking their gum.

Dennie felt their scrutiny as well. She nudged Kessa with her elbow. "We're getting off at the next stop."

The two girls mounted the stairs at the 135th Street station. Kessa surveyed the tired-looking five-story apartment buildings, hoping for Dennie's sake that she lived in a decent place.

The lobby of the building had a scuffed marble floor, but its former elegance still shone through. Dennie led her to the elevator, pressed five, and the noisy door slid shut. As the elevator inched its way up, Kessa noticed different sets of initials scraped into the black enamel paint inside. She realized how spoiled she was to have a doorman who ran the elevator in her own building.

"Five C. The penthouse—ha ha. Here we are."

Kessa looked at the door. "Carré," it read under the doorbell. "How do you pronounce this? I mean, I'm embarrassed because I never even knew your last name."

Dennie smiled. "Yeah. Everybody just calls me Dennie. That's okay. It's pronounced Car-ray. It's French." She took out her keys and opened three locks in the steel door. "Can't be too careful around here," she said casually over her shoulder.

Kessa remembered Tony opening the three locks of his door. That evening seemed so long ago. Deirdre had still been alive then and she hadn't even met Dennie. It was funny how things changed. Funny and sad.

"Mom, we're here."

Mrs. Carré came to the foyer. "You must be Kessa. I'm Celeste Carré."

Kessa smiled nervously at the attractive woman. She was

dressed in a navy blue suit, and her white silk blouse had a large bow tied at her throat. Dressed for success was what the magazines would call it. She seemed warm, curious, and powerful all at once.

"I'm glad to meet you, Mrs. Carré." Kessa continued to smile nervously, thoroughly intimidated and a bit in awe of Dennie's "quotable" mother.

"Won't you excuse me while I change out of my work clothes." She smiled and left the room.

Kessa walked into the living room. It had such a cozy, lived-in feeling to it, with colorful pillows scattered on comfy couches and African wood sculpture adorning the bookshelves. What was the word to describe it? Kessa wondered. Then it came to her. *Character.* The decor had character; it was a visible statement by Dennie's mother.

"Your apartment is so neat."

Dennie smiled proudly. "Yeah, my mom threw out all the European stuff from my father."

Kessa wondered about Dennie's father. Her own father figured so prominently in her life. "Do you see your father often?" she dared to ask.

Dennie frowned and shook her head. She blinked back a few involuntary tears. "No. I haven't seen him since we left Canada."

"It's really nicely decorated," Kessa said hollowly, trying to change the subject.

Dennie continued anyway. "Remember what I said to you in the restaurant about never wanting to pass for white?"

Kessa nodded.

"That's something my mom and I tried in Canada. My father is white, but my mother, my sister, and me can't ever be. It's tougher than getting citizenship, you know. It's actually impossible."

Kessa didn't know what to say. Dennie fingered a statue,

then turned to her friend with a contrite smile. "How about that coffee I promised you?"

"Sure."

"C'mon, I'll show you the kitchen." She led her through a hallway filled with framed portraits and family pictures. Kessa glanced at the smiling faces as she walked by. Her mother didn't hang photos like that.

Dennie got the coffee ready with a casualness that suggested she did this often. She smiled at Kessa's admiration. "I always make the coffee when my mom gets home from work."

"What does your mom do?"

"She's a paralegal."

"What's that?"

"It's a bit like a nurse," Celeste said.

Dennie turned around, surprised at her mother's sudden appearance in the kitchen.

"Hey, what do you mean it's like a nurse?" she protested. "It's nothing like a nurse, Mom."

"Well, it is if you look at the power structure, Dennie."

"I still don't get it."

"Nurses prepare a patient for a doctor, then clean up afterwards. They assist him while he's working as well. I do the same thing for lawyers."

"Is that a good job?" Kessa asked. Though she didn't know it, her naïve question instantly shifted Mrs. Carré away from her anger about the discrepancy in prestige and income between her former husband and herself, between men and women, between lawyers and their assistants. The tension left the room.

"Yes, it's a good job, Kessa. It's challenging, exhausting, and I guess I wish it paid more. We are very ambitious in this house."

Kessa smiled anxiously.

"Dennie, is the coffee ready yet?" Celeste asked.

Dennie automatically looked at the stove. "About two minutes."

Chapter 27

She sat in the rocking chair instead of on the couch. "I felt so strange being in her apartment."

Sherman waited for her to continue.

"I think what made it so strange was her mother. No, it was both of them. I never feel like that when I'm with my mother. They were like a team. They were both annoyed at the same thing, mostly Dennie's father. Her mother seemed tough—not mean, just . . . strong. My mother never seems determined like that. She always seems like she's trying to compromise. Mrs. Carré sounded so definite about everything. I liked that even though she intimidated me. When my mother seems unsure of herself, especially about me, I just feel this rage toward her. I often think I'm looking for reasons to attack her."

"Why do you want to attack her?"

"I don't know. She's really mostly nice to me, never mean or anything. I get the maddest when I think she's being weak about me."

"Is that why you like Mrs. Carré so much?"

"That's got to be it" Kessa was so emphatic she surprised herself. "Dennie would never think of challenging her mother the way I do—and her mother looks like she wouldn't tolerate it for a minute, either. Yeah, Mrs. Carré has something that my mother doesn't."

"Do you think your mother is a weak person?"

"Yes." She hesitated. "No, not with everyone else. I watch her with her friends. She looks so confident, even smooth. She's just not the same with me as she is with them."

"Why do you think she behaves in a weak way toward you? Do you think she's afraid of *you*?"

Kessa sat lost in thought, feeling pangs of guilt for having put her mother down. "Why do I feel responsible for how my mother feels about me?"

"Have you always felt responsible for the way she felt about you—even when you were little?"

"I felt responsible for how everyone in my family related to everyone else."

"Were you active in influencing relationships?"

Kessa smiled as if she were laughing at herself. "I was always nice. 'The best little girl in the world,' my father called me. My being nice might make up for Suzanna's constant arguing with my father. A way of 'influencing relationships,' as you put it."

Sandy nodded. "How do you feel about having the burden, real or imaginary, of keeping the peace at home?"

"Lousy! I tried, and Suzanna got all the attention. I think that the first time they really noticed me was when I lost weight, but that was when I didn't even want them to notice me at all. Now I don't know how I feel about it. I mean, when I see another anorectic on the street I still have doubts and think that I shouldn't have given that up. I get mad thinking my parents don't have to worry about me anymore.

Part of me still wants them to worry." She gave a short laugh. "You remember after our second family therapy session?"

"What would you say to each of them if they were here, Kessa?"

"I wish I could reach out to you . . . but I can't."

Sandy waited for her to continue.

"Wasn't I a good sport for letting you call me crazy?"

He smiled. "You were relieved."

"Yeah, maybe now they'll be nicer to me."

"Maybe, but it won't give you power over them, you know."

"I wish it would. I *am* mad at them, you know?"

"Yes, but if they obey you, it won't lessen your anger."

"What will?"

"When you don't feel like an outsider anymore and they don't feel distant and helpless to you."

"Sometimes I think it's dangerous for me to trust you," Kessa interjected.

"Sometimes it is."

"So why should I?"

"You need to practice on someone."

"Practice what?"

"Practice trusting . . . and taking risks."

"Y'know, Sherman, sometimes you're a smart ass."

"Ah, you're getting tougher too!"

"You are tougher, Kessa, but I wonder what else you want from them aside from worry."

"I can't tell anymore. When I think about it, all I can feel is the anger."

"Do you ever think about boys?"

Kessa looked startled. "Where did that come from?"

"You have so much passion for your parents, yet at your age girls often think about boys. Aside from Tony, you never bring up the subject."

"You're right. I don't want to talk about boys," she stated adamantly.

Sherman waited her out silently, watching her struggle with her thoughts.

"You know, a lot of people have different ideas about men," she said finally. "I mean, there isn't just one idea to have. Dennie and Mrs. Carré, they don't think so much of them. Dennie's father left them both—kicked them out. When Dennie is in school, she can flirt with ten guys at once. Sometimes that makes me jealous. And I feel so inadequate when I'm with her because I think that she knows something about them I don't. She doesn't even care about them, though. She thinks that all guys are big babies—men included. I guess she got that from her mother.

"But men scare me," she continued. "When they look at me, I think they're judging me, inspecting me, maybe wanting something—I never know what. I felt safest when I knew they were thinking of me as a little girl. That's really no good either, because when I want them to take me seriously . . . well, nobody takes a little girl that seriously."

"How do you think about me? Do I belong in any of those categories?"

"I don't like to think about you," Kessa said in a low voice, not meeting his eyes. "When I do, it worries me. You have lots of other patients, and I don't know how much time you ever spend thinking about any of us. I don't feel particularly important here, so I'd rather not talk about it."

There was an awkward silence. He'd meant to encourage her to think about her femininity and now she was actually confronting him, asking him to define how he felt about her.

"So I'm one of those men who don't seem to want anything from you. It seems you can't win."

"What do you mean?" Kessa asked.

"I *do* fit in with your scheme of how men affect you. I'm right there with your father, it seems. Isn't he one of those men who sees you as a little girl? Who won't take you seriously? Aren't you angry at him for not recognizing you in a manner that would make you feel attractive, interesting, effective—potent, even?"

"You're saying that everything I feel has nothing to do with what has happened here, nothing to do with us," Kessa said with a tinge of annoyance in her voice. "You're saying it's all a continuation of my relationship with my father. I resent that."

"Kessa, you may resent it, but you've said that men are a danger to you because they're either predators or neglectors. You've had no positive place to put them in your head. Now, since you've met Dennie, you want to put them in the category of harmless little boys. It's all a way of coping with your fear of them."

"So what am I supposed to do about my fear?"

"I guess if men seem powerful and dangerous to you, it must be in contrast to the lack of power you feel in yourself. You see them as intellectually powerful and sexually dangerous."

She nodded.

"How do you see yourself intellectually and sexually?"

"Intellectually, I pass tests—I'm a good studier—but I never want to discuss anything because I'm afraid people will see how far behind them I am."

"How are you behind?"

"They just know things that I don't. They're comfortable in ways that I'm not. They know how to talk socially about things that I can't."

"Are you talking about men or classes now?"

Kessa shook her head. "No. I'm not talking about men, but they still make me feel the worst. I feel inferior with girls, but guys make me feel scared."

"I guess with guys you're more aware that you're a girl."

She smiled sarcastically. "Whatever that is."

"Then men are mysterious because they highlight how mysterious it is to you to be a woman."

Woman? Kessa raised her eyebrows. She'd never considered herself a woman. Sandy noticed her surprised expression.

"I don't think that I'll ever become a woman," she stated.

"Why not?"

"I just don't feel those things that women feel. I don't like a woman's body—it's fat."

"Is it mysterious?" Sandy asked.

"Is what mysterious?"

"A woman's body."

"What part of a woman's body?"

"Any part."

"Some parts should never be seen." Kessa blushed.

"Even by the owner of the body?"

"Who's the owner of the body?"

"You're the owner of your body."

Kessa had never thought of it that way. "I don't feel like I am."

"Why not?"

"Because I never know what it's going to do. It could gain weight and get fat."

"What else could it do?"

Kessa looked at the carpet. "It could make me get my period."

"Then you would have to cope with it?"

She put one hand over her eyes. "It's like an open wound."

Sandy was overwhelmed into silence by Kessa's comment. *Slowly*, he thought, *I've got to help her come to grips with becoming a woman. But very slowly.* "Who taught you that?" he asked finally.

"What do you mean?"

"Who taught you to see your vagina as an open wound?"

"Do we have to call it by name?" she protested.

"Calling it an open wound is incorrect. I was using the correct name."

"I wasn't calling it by name. I was saying what it looked like."

"I wonder how you learned to see it that way."

"I got my first period when I was twelve. My mother didn't have anything to say, as usual. My father made some crack about how I would have to be careful or I could get pregnant." As she looked at Sherman with accusing eyes, her expression suddenly softened. "You know, I just realized I probably got that lecture about becoming pregnant because my sister'd had an abortion that year." She smiled at her analysis. "But I still think that part of my body is disgusting. Will this kind of talking make that feeling go away?"

"Do you want that feeling of disgust to go away?"

"Yeah, but I'm not so hopeful that it can."

"Maybe we could continue to talk about it until it doesn't feel like such a big deal. Such a big, *bad* deal."

"If it doesn't feel like such a big deal, will I stop being intimidated by men?"

Chapter
28

As the school bell rang for dismissal, Kessa felt a sharp twinge of nerves. Dennie was coming over with her and then after dinner they were going to Skirmishes. That bar made her think of Deirdre. She wondered where Deirdre was. Maybe in heaven she could eat all she wanted and never get fat. Kessa wished she believed that was true.

The skies were gray and leaden as they boarded the bus that would take them across Central Park. Kessa stared out the window at the bleak landscape, barren branches bending in the wind. Though it was March, spring still seemed very far away.

Dennie got off the bus first, and the sharp wind blew her scarf in her face. "Hey!" she laughed. "Kessa, you live on this street, right across from the park?"

"Yeah! But it's the pits in winter. Too bleak." The wind whipped her words.

"Is your mom okay about me coming over for dinner?"

"Sure. It's easier for me. See, this is an integrated neighborhood." Kessa winked.

209

Dennie stuck out her tongue. "I'm sure I deserve that, but spare me the rest, would ya, please."

"I think that can be arranged." Kessa smiled.

Dennie was silent as Charles took them up in the elevator. Grace answered the doorbell.

"Hi, Mom. This is Dennie . . . Dennie, this is my mother."

"Hello, Mrs. Dietrich. Glad to finally meet you in person."

"Yes, it's too bad you two don't live nearer to each other."

Kessa shot an annoyed look at her mother.

Grace bit her lip.

Dennie caught the exchange and wondered what it was all about.

"We'll be in my room for a while, Mom."

"All right. I'll call you when dinner's ready."

Kessa walked quickly to her room, but Dennie lingered behind. She wanted to see the apartment.

"Hey, are we in some kind of rush or something?"

"There's nothing to see. Just a lot of boring furniture. It's not like your house."

"Maybe it's not so boring to me. I mean, do you hate your house?"

"No. I don't hate it, but it's just the place I live in."

"Your mom seems nice to me. Is she putting on an act?"

"No. I guess she's nice, all right," Kessa said grudgingly.

"Yeah, well it looks like her breathing annoys you."

"We just get touchy around each other."

"Well, I—"

"Look! My mom and I don't get along like you and your mom!"

"Okay! Don't bite my head off, please."

"Sorry."

When Grace knocked, Dennie looked reproachfully at the closed door. There were never closed doors in her house. Kessa rushed to open it.

"I just wanted you both to know that dinner will be ready in a few minutes." They had planned the menu a few days before, Grace nearly ecstatic at the mere thought of her daughter's normal dinner party. They decided on lobster tails, salad, and rice, with hot fudge sundaes for desert. Kessa knew it didn't matter what her mother served—she'd be too nervous to eat much of anything.

"Thanks, Mom." Kessa feigned enthusiasm. She didn't want Dennie to think she really hated being a member of the Dietrich family, so she took her on a guided tour of the apartment.

As they approached the dining room, Dennie offered, "Is there anything that I can help you with, Mrs. Dietrich?"

"That's sweet of you, but everything's ready. Just take a seat."

Grace gave a sigh of happiness. Dennie was a lovely girl and seemed perfectly normal. She thought briefly of Kessa's old friend Deirdre, who'd been so . . . well, so anorectic. She pushed those thoughts to the back of her mind.

"Your father has to work late tonight. What are you girls planning for the evening?"

"We're going out," Kessa said flatly.

"Yes, to a sort of teen club."

"That sounds nice, Dennie."

Nicer than me, Kessa thought.

"Kessa, how come your mother is afraid of you?" Dennie asked as they walked into the wind on Central Park West.

"You noticed?"

"Can't miss it."

"I don't know. That's one of the things that's wrong with our relationship."

"You don't even have to help set up dinner."

"It's not such a great deal."

"Oh, it doesn't look like one."

"What do you mean?"

"Don't take me wrong or anything, but you've got no respect for your mother. 'No respect, no security.' That's what my mom says."

Kessa'd had enough of Dennie's quotable mother. It just made her feel worse about herself. "Well, your mom's right, damnit, and I don't want to hear any more about your mom. It's a real pain not having any security, so don't rub it in!"

"Sorry."

"Let's just go to Skirmishes and have a good time. Maybe we'll meet some guys."

"Okay, okay."

Dennie's reply was so deferential that Kessa couldn't believe it. She was actually learning how to assert herself.

But once they were inside Skirmishes, Kessa felt less self-assured. She remembered walking in with Deirdre, talking to Tony, watching Deirdre's emaciated body hurry into the girls' room. It was the last live image she had of her friend. And she remembered how the more confident she pretended to be, the more frightened Deirdre had become.

Now it was different. Dennie looked perfectly at home.

"Let's take that table right in the middle of everything, okay?"

They sat down, Dennie eying all the prospects.

Kessa regarded her friend carefully. Maybe some of Dennie's confidence would rub off on her.

A guy in a well-worn leather bomber jacket turned toward them from the bar. Dennie smiled flirtatiously. Kessa's eyes darted back and forth between the two, watching Dennie draw the boy to their table. Sure enough, he picked up his drink, smiled hesitantly, and walked over to them.

"Can I join you?"

"Sure. My name's Dennie. This is my friend Kessa."

"I'm Brian."

He was about six feet tall, and even in the dim light of the bar Kessa could tell he had wonderful blue eyes. Now that he was at their table, he looked really shy. Dennie noticed Kessa's admiring stare.

"My friend Kessa was interested in meeting you, but she's shy."

Kessa blushed a deep crimson, and Brian looked almost as embarrassed.

Dennie shrugged and stood up. "Sorry, guys. Couldn't resist," she said with a wink. "I'm going to check out the merchandise. See ya later."

Brian saw the look on Kessa's face and forgot his own embarrassment.

"Your friend sure has a lot of self-confidence. Maybe more than both of us."

That comment made her relax a little. "How old are you Brian—really?"

"I'm using my friend's ID here . . . I'm seventeen."

"That's just right. Me too."

"That's funny," Brian said. "Most girls want a guy to be older."

Try to act more like Dennie, Kessa told herself sternly. Aloud, she answered, "Well, *I'm* just not most girls."

They both smiled, then fell silent. *Be more aggressive,* Kessa repeated to herself. "Are you a junior or a senior?" she blurted.

"Well, since you like younger men, I don't mind admitting I'm a junior."

"Me too."

"What are you drinking?"

"Club soda." No calories.

"Do you want me to get you something stronger?"

"No thanks."

"Do you go to school near here?"

"Sure. Isn't Skirmishes for preppies only?"

"Yeah, I guess it is. I go to Lawrence Prep."

"Where's that?"

"Over near the Hudson, in the seventies."

Kessa smiled. "I live not too far from there. Do you live on the West Side too?

"No. I live near here."

"Ah. An East-Sider."

"I don't know why everybody's into this East Side versus West Side stuff," Brian said. "I think it's dumb, but my parents get off on it."

"My father hates the East Side. He says we'd never live there. It's too snobby." Oh God, Kessa thought, what if he thinks I'm a jerk for saying that?

"Your dad's probably right. I don't really like most of my parents' friends."

Kessa sighed in relief. "Who does?"

"Are you as easy to get along with as you seem?"

Was he serious? Kessa blushed again and shrugged. "I don't know . . . I can't tell. Can most people?"

"Can most people what?"

"Can most people tell what others think of them? Can you, Brian?" Kessa couldn't believe how easy it was to talk to him. Dennie must've waved a magic wand or something.

"I think I can. Sometimes. I mean, if you really look at people, you see the expressions on their faces. It's pretty obvious if they like talking to you or not."

"And do you do that with everyone you know?" She put

on a mock serious face. "All right, Brian. How many people are you friends with, and how many of them like you and think you're smart, interesting, and great?" She started laughing at how ridiculous she sounded.

Brian smiled back. "C'mon, Kessa. Most people don't check up on that kind of stuff. I sure don't. I just figure that if somebody's pissed off with me, they'll say so."

"Don't you need to know more than that?"

"Not really. Maybe I'm just an easygoing person. Why, do you?"

Kessa didn't want him to think she was stuck-up or unlikable. "No," she said carefully. "I just like to know where I stand."

"Like with me?"

She quickly shook her head. "No. Just in general."

Too late. He started to laugh. She felt mortified and exposed for an instant, but then Brian reached across the small round table and gently picked up her hand. He traced the lines on her palm. Kessa tried not to shiver.

"Well, Miss Kessa, the fortuneteller says that since you want to know where you stand with me, I'll tell you. You're very pretty, very smart, and very interesting."

"You can't know any of that yet. We just met."

"Ah!" He looked at her palm again. "It also says here that you can't handle a compliment."

"Thanks a lot."

"You also like to talk about deep things, and you hate superficiality."

Kessa couldn't help smiling. His fingers felt warm.

"And I think you like me, too. After all, you have to pay attention to other people's reactions. I just learned that from somebody smart, pretty, and interesting."

Kessa burst into laughter. "All right! I give up! You win!"

"But *what* do I win?"

"I don't know. You tell me, Mr. Know-It-All."

He laughed too. After that it was easy to talk.

Brian suddenly looked at his watch.

"What time do you have to be home, Kessa?"

"Trying to get rid of me already?"

"No. I'm trying to make sure I have enough time to take you home."

"Oh." She thought briefly of Tony. "I, um, you don't need to worry about that. I can get home by myself."

"Maybe I want to worry about that. And maybe I want to take you home—I mean see you home." He blushed.

His embarrassment made her feel almost safe. "Okay, then we should leave now. We can take the crosstown bus."

"I think I can spring for a cab. I'm from the *East Side*, remember?"

"That's nice, but I'm really okay on the bus."

"I'd rather take you home in a cab."

"If that's what you want."

"That's what I want."

"Okay. Let me just say goodbye to Dennie."

The taxi pulled up in front of the Dietrichs' building, and Brian got out quickly to hold the door for Kessa. "Well, aren't we fancy on the West Side," he joked.

"Oh, we do okay on this side of the park."

Brian took her arm. She slowly pulled it away.

"I have to go."

Brian walked her into the lobby and Kessa punched the elevator button.

"Kessa, I, um, I don't know your phone number."

She hesitated for just a second. *Just try,* she told herself sternly.

"Do you have something to write it down with?"

"Sure." He smiled in relief, then dug into all the pockets of his jacket and pants before he found a pen and a cleaning receipt. He wrote down the number as Charles stood guard, a proprietary smile hovering on his face.

"Well." Brian looked a little nervous. "Gotta go. I'll call you tomorrow." He gave a quick smile and hurried out the door.

Chapter
29

"So you had a good time?" Sherman couldn't help sounding pleased.

"But it didn't help. After he left, all I thought about for the next two hours—and it was already midnight when I got home—was how many stupid things I said to him. Then I started feeling fat. Every time I think about him, I feel fat!"

"Do you like him?"

"Yeah. I like him, but I feel fat."

"What does liking him have to do with feeling fat?"

Kessa shrugged. Sandy pressed the point. "You haven't talked about feeling fat in quite a while."

"Well maybe I haven't, but that doesn't mean I don't."

"Are you mad at me because you feel fat?"

"I'm just mad."

"Does Brian scare you?"

"Of course he does. I don't know anything about having a relationship, or even why I should have one. And I don't even know what I want to happen."

"Even though you don't know why, you seem to want a relationship—especially this one—nonetheless."

"I don't know what I want. I never know what I want!" Kessa yelled.

"What frightens you the most?"

"The whole thing. It's so unfamiliar that I can't even look at it closely enough to decide what scares me."

"Does he seem nice?"

"Yes, but that doesn't matter. You don't understand how . . . how . . . retarded I am! I don't know how to cope. I mean, my fears aren't the fears *you'd* probably expect me to have. God." She had to make him understand. "How would you like to run a hospital on Mars, and all your patients are Martians, of course. So, Dr. Sherman, what would *you* be most afraid of? After all, *you* are a doctor. And a hospital is a hospital, even if it's on Mars."

"All right, Kessa. I see your point."

"Well if you do, then tell me what you'd be afraid of."

"Of not knowing anything about it. Failing, courting disaster, harming others, being harmed myself, being condemned, being in an alien place."

"So!" Kessa was proud of her analogy. "Now, Dr. Sherman, you're beginning to see my point. Except what's so humiliating for me is that my fears are about doing what everybody knows how to do already. Like have a relationship! When you met me I didn't even know how to eat, so I've made some progress, haven't I? Huh, Dr. Sherman?"

Sherman knew he deserved her chastisement, and mixed in with his professional embarrassment was a real pride in Kessa's ability to argue. "You're right. I apologize for not realizing how overwhelming the idea of a relationship is to you. I wonder, though, if you've noticed how much you cope with *our* relationship. It may be structured, but it's still real. You coped with me about all the toughest issues in your life.

You've been pleased with some things I've said and hated others. Yet you're still here right now, coping with your disappointment in me—and fully capable of letting me have it."

"But I hate it when you don't understand me. If you don't understand what I'm going through, then I think it can't ever be fixed."

"If you expect me to know everything, Kessa, you'll be disappointed. Of course I wish I *did* know everything."

"So where does that leave me? I mean, how can you help me stay in a relationship? What if I'm never able to have one?"

"If you decide to pursue your relationship with Brian, I'm afraid that it's going to have to be pretty self-conscious."

"Oh, that's just great! Everything that I do with people is already self-conscious."

"But this one will be different in the *way* it's self-conscious. Instead of just accusing yourself of behaving inadequately, you'll have to analyze how Brian affects you, what you say to him, and how he reacts to you."

"Oh boy! Sounds like the love affair of the century!"

"Well, it might even become that." Sandy smiled and leaned back in his chair. "But not without a lot of work on your part." He hesitated. "Kessa, a minute ago you were furious with me. Now you aren't. Do you know why?"

"No I don't," she lied. Sandy was pissing her off. But she knew why. "Because I think you are right."

"Perhaps it would be a good idea if we practiced analyzing your relationships here."

"What do you mean?"

"We should understand what happens in here between us."

"But that's different. This isn't like anyplace else."

"Sure it is. The way you deal with me is the way you deal

with other important people in your life. What happens when you blow up at your mother the way you just did with me?"

"My mother's much nicer than you. She tries to calm me down and understand why I'm angry. And you know what? It's weird. When she does that—when I know she's trying to be nice—I just get madder and meaner to her."

"Why?"

"I don't know. She gets me so mad that I have to let it out. I feel guilty afterward, but I never apologize."

"Do you ever do that with your father?"

"Hah! He'd kill me if I looked at him funny."

"Then you feel different toward him than you do toward your mother?"

"You know I do. But they each feel different about me. My mother's afraid of me. She loves me and everything . . . and I know it's strange . . . but I think *she* thinks I'm smarter than she is."

"Does your father think you're smarter than he is?"

"My father thinks I'm an idiot." She giggled.

"Does he really?"

"Who knows. I could never tell what he thinks of me. He never makes me feel particularly good."

"What does he tell you about yourself? Does he tell you that you're pretty? Does he seem interested in you . . . in what you have to say?"

Kessa shook her head. "I don't think he really thinks very much of me. When I'm with him, I always feel like he's checking up on me and that what he finds disappoints him. Like he doesn't know me at all."

"Does he have a lot of prestige in your eyes?"

"I really don't like that question." She sat quietly for a minute. "I hate it because I don't think I'll ever hear anything good about myself from my father. He only thinks about me when he has to worry about something. I don't know what I could ever do that would impress him."

"Would you like to impress him?"

She began to nod, and her eyes filled with tears. She'd tried so hard to get his approval—she'd have done anything. "You know, if he actually did compliment me for something, I'd probably croak from the shock."

"You don't really accept compliments from your mother, either."

"But I can always get compliments from my mother. She'd say anything to calm me down. Daddy just gets annoyed. I always hear him complaining about the people who work for him. He'll always talk about someone he's going to fire. He never has anything good to say about the employees in his company. If he could, he'd probably fire me."

"I guess you'd rather have a promotion, and a raise?"

She smiled bitterly. "It's funny. I get all the promotions and raises I could want from my mother, so I resent her for being so easy. Daddy doesn't give me that, but I still really believe him. If he doesn't see me as special, it makes me sure that he's right. You could tell me wonderful things the way my mother does, but you're probably supposed to. I can't ever get as mad at you as I do with my mother because you don't let me."

"How did your father get so much more prestige in your eyes than your mother?"

"He took it."

"What do you mean? Did he take it from your mother?"

"Maybe she just gave it to him. I guess she figured that she was supposed to."

"How did she do that?"

"If I had a homework problem, she would always say, 'Ask your father. He knows more about that than I do.'

When I started high school, she would even say to me that I was 'brighter' than she was. But if she makes me believe that, who will I have to turn to?"

"Who *do* you have to turn to?"

"Nobody! Oh there's a few, I guess, but it doesn't feel like it."

"How do you cope with me?"

She raised her eyebrows. "It's not easy! Sometimes you sound like my mother and that's when I get mad at you. But when I do, you don't act like my mother would, so that makes me afraid. So then I worry that you'll turn into my father—but you don't, well ... maybe a little—yet when you sound like him, you're never as scary as he really is."

"When do I sound like her?"

"When you're nice. When I feel like you care about me."

"Is that when you get mad at me?"

"Sometimes."

"Then you think that kindness is the same as weakness?"

"Sort of feels that way, doesn't it?"

"Well, it doesn't look like you get to accept much kindness from anyone. It's a lot like the way you dealt with food when you were emaciated. You always wanted food, but if you ate, you felt bad."

"So how many other ways am I crazy? I can't stand it sometimes. As soon as we get past the biggest problem, we—excuse me, *I*—have—here's another whopper!"

" 'We' is all right. Your problems are *our* problems."

"But *you* don't have to live with them."

"No, I don't. But I'd like to help you out of all this."

"So how many more problems will I, or *we*, discover now?" she asked sarcastically.

"Kessa, this was never just about eating and weight."

Kessa rolled her eyes at the ceiling. Sometimes Sandy Sherman was a royal pain.

Chapter
30

Kessa's room looked like a tornado had hit it. Clothes were piled all over the place as she tried on nearly every outfit in her closet. Nothing seemed right. Either it was too girlish or too boring or ... it made her look too fat.

She finally decided on a hand-knit Irish fisherman's sweater and cropped jeans. Casual but nice.

Now for the makeup. Kessa went to the bathroom and stared at her face. She wasn't too good at putting stuff on, but she certainly wasn't going to ask her mother for advice. Dennie, she thought. Remember to ask Dennie for a makeup lesson next week.

Kessa sucked in her cheeks and put on a little blush, remembering how hollow her cheeks used to be. She picked up a tube of lipstick. Peach melba, it said. What a dumb name, Kessa thought as she carefully outlined her lips. Then a terrible thought hit her. What if Brian tried to kiss her— would he get lipstick on his mouth? Would he not want to kiss her if she wore lipstick?

Kessa blotted nearly all of it off, wishing for once that

Suzanna were around. Suzanna sure knew enough about kissing. Well, that was another item to add to the list of questions for Dennie.

The bell rang, and Grace hurried to the door. It was Kessa's first date with Brian, and she'd been locked in her room for nearly two hours already. Grace was as excited for Kessa as she was worried that the evening might not be a success. The fear of a relapse was always at the back of her mind. She opened the door, hoping the young man wouldn't look too scruffy—or worse, too old.

"Hello, Mrs. Dietrich. I'm Brian."

"Hello, Brian. It's a pleasure to meet you. Please come in." Grace smiled in pure pleasure. *He's perfect*, she thought. *Handsome, not too old, a boyish grin, nicely dressed, just the right sort of boy for my daughter*. Grace had always seen her daughter's illness as a personal attack, and now she saw this charming, very acceptable boy almost as a present from Kessa. *Look, Mom, Francesca Louise Dietrich can go out on dates like all the other girls. I'm not a freak—I was just kidding. And you're the best mom in the whole world*.

Brian sat in the Dietrichs' living room, nervously trying to look casual. Kessa poked her head into the room.

"Hi, Brian. Ready?"

"Sure."

Kessa went to the hall closet, pulled out her coat, and hurried to the front door. Brian nearly ran to catch up with her.

"Goodbye Kessa," Grace called. She entered the foyer just as Kessa was about to close the door.

"Oh goodbye, Mom. Um, we're a bit late. See you later."

"Are you mad at your mother?" Brian asked while they waited for the elevator.

"Not especially. I just didn't want to get into a chummy conversation on our way out."

"Yeah, that can be awkward."

When they got to the lobby, Brian asked hesitantly, "We'll go straight to the movies and then eat something afterward, right?"

Kessa nodded. "Sorry, but I'm really not hungry now."

"No sweat. What do you want to see?"

"*West Side Story* is up at the Thalia. I've seen it before, but I really like it. Is that okay?" *I want to be like Maria,* she thought, *I want to feel pretty.*

"Sounds great. And you know what—I've never seen it."

"Must be 'cause you're from the *East* Side."

"Very funny, Miss Dietrich."

"What an ending," Brian said, turning to Kessa. He was about to ask her how she felt when he noticed the tears streaming down her face. "Would you like a tissue?" He frantically searched his pockets, knowing he would probably come up empty. She shook her head in response, mortified that she couldn't stop crying. He'd think she was a total baby and take her home and never call her again.

Brian felt awful. He put his arm around her, but she drew back.

"I'm okay," she reassured him, smiling weakly to take the sting out of refusing his arm. "I always cry at movies. Even *Bambi* and *Mary Poppins.*"

Brian smiled back, but she could still tell how rejected he felt. "Do you want to go out to eat now?" he asked her.

"Sure, there're some nice places around here." She stood up and touched his sleeve gently. His smile widened.

Kessa made it through her plain quiche and salad with no major panic attack. After the coffee had been set down, she put her hands self-consciously near her cup. Brian reached across the small table and took one of her hands, tracing his finger gently over her palm as he'd done in Skirmishes. Only this time it was a gesture of real affection, not teasing. Again she wanted to pull back, more out of embarrassment than fear. Kessa simply wasn't used to it. What might have appeared to an onlooker as a whisper of innocent friendship felt to Kessa like a deafening roar of undeserved praise. The more tempting it was to enjoy the pressure of Brian's fingers, the more frightened she felt.

"Kessa, I—"

She couldn't bear to hear anything, and pulled her hand away.

"I was going to say that I really like you. I didn't mean to make you nervous."

"I guess I'm not so good at having my hand held." She had to try to explain her behavior to Brian. Otherwise he'd think she was a jerk and didn't really like him.

"Maybe I could help you get better at it."

His offer felt so generous that she became dizzy for a moment, and she bit the inside of her lip so she wouldn't burst into tears. She took a deep breath. "Maybe you could."

"I want to run and hide, yet I want him to know who I am, to hide nothing from him."

"Will you see him again?"

"Next Saturday." She looked at him suspiciously. "Don't you think I should? *I* think I should. He asked me out . . . and I want to."

"Why do you want to?"

"Because he's nice . . . and he's cute . . . and he doesn't scare me too much, and he says I'm nice." *Nice.* Kessa thought with a pang about Deirdre. She remembered calling her and provoking her "niceness." But that was different. That was fake nice. This was real.

Sherman didn't respond. She knew he was waiting for her to finish.

"I . . . um . . . I'm tired of running from everyone who isn't intimidated by me. I want somebody other than you to know me. And Dennie. But she's a girl. I mean, I used to be so surprised that someone like Dennie would want *me* for a friend. But we're so used to each other now, and she's got her own hangups too. I'm really lucky she's my friend. I just hope that Brian won't run when he gets to know me."

"It's risky."

"And I hate risks! You know that."

"Other people are always risks."

"Are you trying to talk me out of this or what?"

"I guess I'm trying to show you how much you've grown. In the past you wouldn't have even considered taking such a risk. Now you do it and complain about it . . . but you do it."

"I wish I felt brave."

"Do you know how a brave person feels?"

"How?"

"Scared."

She smiled, then laughed. "Well then, I'm definitely brave." She laughed some more, then stared at the floor.

Sandy recognized the look. "Seems like you have a tough question to ask."

She nodded.

"Since there are no mind readers available today, I guess you'll have to ask it out loud."

"Just give me a minute or two. . . . How come . . . when Brian held my hand, it made me really tense," she said hesitantly. "When he put his arm around me on the street, I felt stiff. He even gave me a real quick kiss good night and I thought my lips would go numb. I was petrified. All that stuff . . . what you call affection, romance even, it just makes me tense up."

"What do you think of what he did?"

"It was all right. It's not that I didn't like the idea of what he was doing, but I want to be able to feel less creepy when he does it. Does everybody feel this creepy?"

"I guess if it's new or forbidden."

"Nobody ever told me it was forbidden. Hmm." She looked pensive. "But it does feel that way, you know. I haven't the faintest clue how to respond. I've always been a problem hugger." She smiled at the phrase. "I just stand there, not knowing what to do with my arms or anything. When my parents did hug me, it always felt like they were really uncomfortable, like they were doing it because they were supposed to. I don't want to feel that way anymore."

Sherman smiled. "I guess you're going to need lots of practice to get used to it."

"What if it doesn't work? What if Brian thinks I'm a cold fish or something?"

"Then you'll lose him."

"Why did you say that?"

"It was the only honest answer to your question."

"Well, why should I try if I might lose?"

"Because if you don't try, you are *guaranteed* to lose."

Kessa smacked the couch with her fist. "It's not fair. I don't want to lose . . . or to fail."

"Take a chance."

"I hate taking chances! I still want to control everything."

"And you still don't trust yourself to cope with disappointment?"

"I don't trust myself to do anything right."

"Then everything is more difficult."

"Thanks for the information! You know, once you invited me to be scared with you. I thought you were crazy when you first said that. It was the worst invitation anyone ever gave me. This is what you meant, isn't it?"

He nodded.

"Why is it so hard for me to be scared?"

"Because you're always scared alone. You never feel like you have anybody to fall back on. It's easier to be scared if you feel there are people behind you, supporting you."

"But I don't trust anyone."

"That's not entirely true."

"What do you mean?"

"You trust me, Kessa."

She stared at the floor again. Did she? Did she trust Dennie too? She decided she didn't, even though she was her best friend, because she still couldn't confide in her about anorexia.

"I guess you don't want me to know that you trust me."

She shrugged.

"I think it's fine that you trust me."

"Well, you're not a regular person in my life. Forty-five-minute therapy isn't real life. You talk to lots of people. I'm not the only one."

"You don't have to be the only one for it to be real. Besides, all this talk about therapy is a way for you to find it acceptable to trust me. If I offered to see you any time you wanted—without an appointment—the lack of boundaries would terrify you."

"Try me!" she exclaimed. "Well, I don't want so many boundaries, as *you* put it, with Brian."

"That's progress."

She stuck out her tongue. "I still wanna know why I feel tense every time he touches me."

"I don't know. What would you rather feel?"

"Well, what do other girls feel when guys touch them?"

He hesitated. "Cared for, desired, aroused."

"I don't get it. I mean, I know what 'cared for' means; but about the other two?"

Her naïveté almost made him smile. "Desired means he thinks you're pretty and he wants to be romantic with you."

"What about aroused?"

"It means to have feelings awakened in you."

"The only feelings that are awakened in me are tension and fear. Is that what you mean?"

"No, I was referring to sexual feelings."

"Just from holding my hand?" she protested.

"Is that a scary idea?"

"It makes me feel pretty uneasy. Do you think maybe I feel tense because I might feel . . . aroused . . . if I didn't feel tense?"

"How do you feel about being aroused?"

"Creepy!" She looked thoughtful. "Does that mean that I'm frigid or something?"

"I don't think there's any such thing as frigid. Just confused or conflicted. It does take a while to accept new ideas about yourself, you know."

"Will I get better about all this before Brian gets bored or turned off by me? I mean, I'm really far behind other girls my age."

"You know what I'm about to say?"

"Yes, damnit." She mimicked him: "It's risky!"

He nodded. "If he's patient, he'll wait around."

"What if I'm not worth waiting for?"

"I think we'll make the most progress, Kessa, if we're *both* on your side."

"Yeah, well part of me is still waiting for you to discover who I *really* am. I still think I've got you fooled, and when you find out, you won't like me anymore."

"Maybe you have *yourself* fooled about who you really are."

"Well, if I'm Little Miss Fabulous, how come my parents never knew it? They always focused on my sister. I was always the boring one. And they've known me all my life."

"How do you know they haven't found you interesting or smart?"

"I'd just know it."

"Maybe they thought that you didn't need to be told, that it might give you a swelled head."

"No way. You're making excuses for them. Especially my father."

"You're right."

"So how am I supposed to feel better about myself?"

Kessa's vulnerability always touched his heart. "By trusting other people who will teach you new things about yourself."

"More risk, huh? I swear, you're going to have me running for president one of these days."

Chapter
31

I need a walk, Kessa decided. She headed down Madison Avenue. It was lined with trendy boutiques selling designer clothes. She inspected different window displays. It suddenly dawned on her that she never really looked at clothes. Or who was wearing them. When she'd been really thin, she'd only thought about how clothes would make her look fat. Now she wanted clothes to make her look good. She eyed the women passing by. Many had fur coats on. How much did furs cost? Kessa looked down at her own well-worn down jacket. Functional but shapeless. A beautiful woman passed by in a snug leather jacket with matching leather pants. She just looked so . . . well, so chic. And she flaunted it. How'd she know how to pull herself together? Kessa wanted to know that lady's secrets about womanhood. She wanted all these women to tell her. Sherman could tell her *about* it. He could ask her questions to help her find out, but where was the *woman* who would share her secrets?

She noticed two men unloading furniture from a truck. They seemed to be father and son. As an elegantly dressed woman—Kessa noticed the beautiful shape of her legs, how sexy they looked in high heels—navigated around them, they both stopped for an instant, tracking her with their eyes. The woman crossed the street and out of their view, but Kessa saw how other heads turned. At first she was annoyed by the gawking—she knew how humiliating the stare of a stranger could be—but then in a sort of perverse way she became jealous of the younger man. At least he had someone to pass on the secret to him. Someone who, with a wink of his eye, a nudge of his elbow, could indicate to him what was acceptable for men to do, at least.

She tried to imagine standing on a street corner with her mother. A handsome man passes them. Her mother turns to her, nodding in approval. It seemed so absurd!

Kessa stomped down the street, furious with her mother. She tried to imagine Grace behaving seductively. She couldn't. She tried to imagine what her mother had been like when she'd dated Harold twenty-five years ago. She couldn't. Had anyone passed the secret on to her mother?

Kessa walked off her anger. She stopped in front of a shoe store, thinking of the elegant woman in her high heels. Kessa had never even tried high heels on. Tempting, but not today. Not till she knew more secrets.

As she turned away, she saw a man picking up his toddler, who had tripped on the pavement. He kissed her cheek even though it was her knee that hurt. He hugged her until she stopped crying. Kessa tried to remember the last time her father had hugged her. A problem hugger, she'd said. She wondered what daughters were supposed to get from their fathers. Did the secret come from them? Her sister Suzanna got yelled at a lot, but she also got smiles and shared laughter from her father while Kessa got nothing. Even Gregg, selfish egomaniac Gregg, got all the accolades and pats on the back. Maybe that was why he was such a jerk. No one—except Kessa—had ever told him he wasn't.

She looked at her reflection in a gallery window. Was she pretty? Would she feel pretty, like Maria? All she could see was a bewildered, awkward teenager. She wanted to ask someone, anyone, even a stranger, what she looked like. She began to feel fat. She hated that feeling, but at least it felt like something concrete to hang on to. Everything else was so vague.

An attractive man in his twenties was walking toward her, a smile hovering on his lips. She nearly went up to him to ask him why he was smiling, but she could never approach a stranger like that. What did men think about all the time? She hoped Brian would keep liking her.

Brian. She liked him so much—his blue eyes, his smile, his dirty-blond hair. And he had a nice body too, and a firm butt. Dennie was always rating men according to how good their butts were. But the thought of getting physically close still made her really tense. Hugging had repelled her for as long as she could remember. Kissing was a possibility, perhaps, but anything more seemed unthinkable.

Kessa walked into a coffee shop and sat at a booth in the back. The place was nearly deserted at five in the afternoon. As she shrugged off her down jacket and looked down at the menu on the table, she noticed the shape of her breasts through her sweater. For the past two years she had hated having them. They were all that boys noticed. She used to think that they were just lumps of fat. She remembered a party three years before. It was dark and everyone was sprawled out across the furniture. This guy from school reached around and cupped her breast with his hand. She remembered staring down at his hand, wondering what he was getting out of it. She just felt squeezed and mishandled.

She turned to him and said, "Do you mind?" He was startled and apologetically pulled his hand away. "I thought you'd like that," he protested. "Maybe if we knew each other better," she bullshitted, hoping that answer was appropriate. She couldn't actually imagine a circumstance where she would enjoy being touched like that at all.

Kessa looked down at her breasts again and smiled. Now she was curious about them. About her body. She wanted to know its secrets. And she hoped that something, someone, somehow would make her feel "aroused," awakened in some new way. Then maybe she would know their secrets too.

Later that evening, she locked the door to her room. Quickly, she undressed and sat on the edge of her bed, looking shyly at her body in the mirror. There were no awkwardly protruding bones. She was tempted to berate herself for becoming fat, but she didn't. She liked her muscles from gymnastics. Her world had become larger than simply a contest between herself and her body, she realized, reveling in the idea. More than judging how her figure appeared at any set weight, she now worried about its acceptability, its desirability. Parts of her body made her afraid, yet this fear was almost fascinating. She stood up and stretched her arms toward the ceiling. *I'm rising to the challenge*, she told herself. *Literally. After all, everyone's got these parts. I guess I've got to accept mine.*

There was a knock at the door.

"Yes?" Kessa sat down.

"Kessa, dinner's ready in ten minutes, but your father'll be late. Can I come in?"

"I'm not dressed."

"So what?"

"Oh, let me get a robe. . . ."

Kessa opened the door. "You know, Mom, when you just

said that—you not caring if I was dressed or not—I realized that I've never seen you undressed."

"Never?"

"Well, we're not exactly casual about that sort of thing around here."

"Do you think that's wrong, dear?"

"Mom, are you comfortable with your body?"

Grace blushed. "Well, I suppose I wish it were a bit younger."

"Did you ever talk about this kind of stuff with Suzanna?"

"Your sister asked me to take her to a gynecologist. Is that what you mean?"

"No. I mean did you and Suzanna ever talk about you?"

"Well, uh, no. Were we supposed to?"

"Well, I don't know. But how are girls supposed to know if they're normal and stuff?"

"Oh, I'm sure that you're normal, Kessa."

"How can you be sure? I don't know what normal looks like."

"Do you want to see a gynecologist?"

"No! I just wanted to talk to you about what girls are supposed to know."

Grace was getting nervous. She never felt comfortable talking about her body. Some women talked about their sex lives all the time, but not Grace. It was too private, too . . . intimate. "I'm not sure what you want to know."

"I want to know how we're supposed to feel about ourselves and guys . . . men."

"With the right man, you're supposed to feel fine."

"Fine?! What do you mean, fine? What about aroused?"

Aroused? This conversation was getting far too explicit. Grace couldn't think of what to say. "Um . . . that too, dear."

"Who gives us permission to be aroused?"

"Permission? I never thought about it that way. I suppose we have to give ourselves permission."

"Do you give yourself permission, Mother?"

"Well . . . I'm not sure what you want me to say. This is not the kind of thing one talks about."

Please tell me, Mom, Kessa begged silently. *I need to know your secrets.* "I just wanted to know if you've given yourself permission."

"Well, I suppose I must have."

"Mom, is it something you're not ever supposed to tell me about?" *Please don't say no. Please tell me.*

"No, not at all. It's just, well . . . I'm afraid it's something I don't know how to tell you about."

"But you know about it. So why can't you teach me?"

"Teaching was never my strong point. Your father—"

"Don't tell me how my father was the better teacher! Or the better anything!"

"Don't talk that way about your father, Kessa."

"I'm not talking about my father! I'm talking about the way *you* talk about him! You always put *him* on a pedestal—and yourself down. It doesn't look like such a good deal for you."

"I'm happy as—"

"As second-class?" Kessa interrupted.

"I don't see why I have to defend myself to you. Why are you being so nasty to me?"

Kessa burst into tears of frustration. "Mom, I'm so angry with you. I'm sorry. I wish that I could be angry at you without feeling so guilty."

Grace summoned up her own nerve to confront her daughter. "What do you want from me?"

Kessa looked at the floor, brushing tears away with the

back of her hand. "I guess I want you to be stronger than me. I want you to teach me things . . . but I don't know what."

"Oh, Kessa, you've always been reluctant to learn from me. You were always the kid who wanted to do it herself. You didn't even like the instruction booklets that came with toys—all you ever said was, 'I'd rather figure it out myself.' You've never let me teach you anything."

"I guess I was always too tough to handle," Kessa said ruefully.

"No, on the contrary—you were too *easy* to handle. You never needed handling. You *did* always do it yourself, and you did it right. Why should I have interfered with your success?"

"I don't know! I don't understand anything," Kessa burst out. Her mother was just getting off too easily. "I don't even know how to react when a guy holds my hand. I hope I can figure it out for myself, because I guess it's just another one of those things that you can't—or won't—teach me."

"Well, nobody ever taught me!" Grace protested. "That's just something we might have to learn for ourselves."

Kessa opened her mouth in amazement. So that really *was* it. No one had told her mother the secret, either. No wonder she was so hung up about it. Kessa nearly started to laugh. She couldn't be angry or blame her mother anymore. "Never mind, Mom. I'm just a little nervous 'cause of Brian." *I'll either figure it out for myself or find someone else to teach me.*

Grace eagerly accepted Kessa's explanation. "I'm sure he likes you."

"Is dinner ready?"

That was a question Grace could answer. She looked at her watch. "Just about," she said, and hurried into the kitchen.

Story of my life, Kessa thought. *Just about*. Just about to grow up. Just about to be free.

Chapter
32

Shopping can actually be fun, Kessa thought as she cruised slowly through the aisles in Bloomingdale's. She'd decided it was time for a major wardrobe overhaul and smugly recalled the look of shocked delight on Grace's face when Kessa asked to borrow her charge card. Grace had nearly dropped her wallet, she'd been so excited.

Kessa walked into the lingerie department. First things first. She felt a twinge of self-consciousness when a saleslady approached and politely inquired if she needed any help, but Kessa shook her head and said she was just looking. Other women were combing the racks, pulling out and admiring panties and bras they liked. Two girls about her own age were giggling as they gossiped about the guys in their school. One of the girls held a pair of skimpy black lace panties against her jeans. "Well, what d'ya think?" she asked her companion.

"Oh, Lizzie, he'll *love* it," the other girl gushed, and they both laughed.

Lizzie put them back. "Forget it. If he wants to see them, *he* can buy them."

Kessa's eyes widened in shock. I'm not quite ready for *that*, she thought.

She looked at a rack of plain cotton bras, devoid of any ornamentation. Just like the one she was wearing. *Just like me,* she thought.

She moved on to another rack, then fingered the lovely garments in delight. They were just what she wanted. Delicate pink, subtly feminine without being too sexy. Not sure of her size, Kessa pulled off a few to try on. The saleslady directed her to the dressing room, and Kessa peeled out of her clothes. *I'm anxious to see what I look like—I want to see my body,* she thought, *I want to really see it.* The dusky rose of the undies made her skin look very pale and fresh. Kessa stared at herself in the long mirror. *"I have a nice figure,"* she said softly, amazed. She touched her flat tummy, saw the layers of muscles strengthened from gymnastics. *I'm not fat! I'm not fat anywhere!*

She got dressed in a daze, then hurried back to the rack where she'd found the matching set. They had it in other colors, too. Kessa liked it so much she picked out the same thing in lilac, beige, and powder blue.

"You're really wise to buy lots of something you like," the saleslady confided as she wrapped up Kessa's purchases. "Whenever I find something *I* like, I *always* tell myself to buy *lots* of them, but I never do. And then I could *kick* myself afterwards. Enjoy!" Kessa took the bag proudly and headed for the junior department.

She walked from rack to rack, observing the chattering girls hanging out there as she'd done in the lingerie department. She wished for a minute that Dennie was with her, but she knew she had to find her own style—*herself*. Jeans, ski pants, big sweaters, oversize shirts. I don't want anything baggy, Kessa decided. I want to show off my real body. She remembered how she used to flaunt her gaunt skeletal frame, reveling in the shocked stares of strangers. Not anymore, ever again!

Then she spotted just what she wanted. Knits. Soft and clingy, but not too obvious. There was a skirt and sweater set in the softest shade of mauve. The sweater had a V in front, but it wasn't too revealing, and the skirt was tight till it flared out in gentle pleats just below the knee. It was sensational. Kessa knew it would fit even before she tried it on.

Shoes came next. Kessa didn't care if she drove the salesclerk crazy when she picked up every shoe on display. She had to find the right pair. She felt like Cinderella going to the ball.

When at last she settled on a sleek pair of beige pumps with inch-and-a-half heels, Kessa knew she was almost finished. The last stop was hosiery. She recalled the woman she'd seen that chilly afternoon on Madison Avenue. The elegant woman with the beautiful legs and sexy high heels. Well, Kessa's heels weren't quite so high, but she was going to get the sheerest, most divine pair of pantyhose ever made. And then she'd feel sexy too.

When the doorbell rang at six, Kessa hurried to answer it. "I'll get it, Mom!" she called.

As Grace came into the foyer to greet Brian, she noticed Kessa's new outfit.

"Hello, Mrs. Dietrich. Hi, Kessa," he said. "You look really nice."

Kessa blushed just a little. Brian's admiration made her feel all tingly inside. For the very first time in her life, she felt the power she could have as a woman. The power and the joy.

"Hi yourself. I'll be ready to leave in a sec. Mom, I want to show you something." She pulled her mother into the bathroom and shut the door. Then she pulled up her sweater, flaunting her new pink bra. "Well, what do you think?"

Grace smiled. "Very good taste, and sexy too."

Kessa pulled down her sweater and then hiked up her skirt.

"Bravo!" Grace laughed when she saw the matching lace bikini. "Good taste, sexy—and the brains to match!"

"You know, Mom," Kessa said as she checked her appearance in the mirror. "I don't feel like I own these yet. I feel like I borrowed them from someone more grown-up. But I know I'm going to grow into them soon." With that, she gave her mother a hug—so brief that Grace didn't have time to react. And then she was gone.

Kessa couldn't wait to get outside. The sky was darkening, but a teasing hint of spring filled the air.

"Well, where to, Miss Dietrich?" Brian asked. He stood on Central Park West, smiling his usual hesitant smile, his hands scrunched in his pants.

"Let's just walk for a bit and then decide," Kessa said. She felt like running down the street, screaming at the top of her lungs: *I feel good! I'm me, Kessa, and I'm okay!*

Brian tuned in to her mood right away. "Looks like you just won a gold medal."

"I feel like I did. I feel like I won—like I beat myself after all."

Brian looked a little perplexed.

"Sorry," Kessa said. "I'm just being silly." Now wasn't the time for explanations. But that was just how she felt: She *had* defeated herself—her old self, the old scared

Kessa. The thinner wasn't the winner anymore. *This* Kessa was.

"I like you being silly," Brian said shyly.

Kessa took a deep breath, then stuck her hand in his pocket and entwined her fingers in his. His hand felt warm and soft—a little scary, but she got used to it. He smiled at her so sweetly that she forgot to be tense.

"Thanks," he said, so softly she hardly heard it.

"Any time," she replied. "Any time at all."

An Afterword by the Author

Kessa is a work of fiction, but there are many thousands of girls like Kessa in real life. It is to these girls, to their parents and their friends, that I would like to speak now.

Since the publication of *The Best Little Girl in the World*, in which the character Kessa first appears, I have received hundreds of letters from readers who recognized in themselves, or in their friends or loved ones, the signs of anorexia nervosa. Unfortunately, there are not enough hours in the day to answer all of these letters personally, but I have read them all carefully. So, to all those thoughtful readers who have written me, this book is my answer.

I imagine this story may raise questions as well. The answers, I hope, will come not so much from experts as from dialogues within the family—between mothers and daughters, husbands and wives, fathers and daughters. Where such conversations are not possible, or not enough, outside help is needed. There are several organizations that specialize in helping victims of eating disorders, which you will find listed below.

Not so long ago, no one had ever heard about anorexia nervosa or bulimia. Perhaps some day they will be part of the past. Currently, though, they are getting so much attention that an adolescent girl who identifies with Kessa's pain may think that she too must follow Kessa's long and tortuous route through this disease in order to justify receiving help. This is not true. Kessa's relief from her pain came when she was *beginning to free herself* from her obsession with thinness. It was only then that the other issues were discernable and she could begin to grow.

For those of you who are not suffering from anorexia nervosa yet who identify with Kessa, what you have in common with her goes much deeper than a problem of eating or thinness. You are striving to become a woman in a complex society that makes it difficult to understand what it is to be a woman. Whatever that may be for you, it will surely be more than a question of weight and appearance.

—S.L.

Organizations that assist victims of anorexia and bulimia:

American Anorexia/Bulimia Association
John Atchley, M.D., President
133 Cedar Lane
Teaneck, New Jersey 07666
201-836-1800

National Anorexia Nervosa and Associated Disorders
Vivian Meehan, R.N., President
Box 271
Highland Park, Illinois 60035
312-831-3438

ANAS
Patricia Warner, President
Box 213
Lincoln Center, Mass. 07773
617-259-9767

Center For The Study of Anorexia/Bulimia
William David, Ph.D., Director
1 West 91st Street
New York, New York 10024
212-595-3449